The Conf[usions of]

Young Ma[ster Törless]

Robert [Musil]

Translated by Christopher Moncrieff

ALMA CLASSICS

Contents

ALMA CLASSICS LTD
London House
243-253 Lower Mortlake Road
Richmond
Surrey TW9 2LL
United Kingdom
www.almaclassics.com

The Confusions of Young Master Törless first published in German in 1906
This edition first published by Alma Classics Ltd in 2013

Translation © Christopher Moncrieff, 2013

Cover © nathanburtondesign.com

Printed and bound by CPI Group (UK) Ltd, Croydon, CR0 4YY

ISBN: 978-1-84749-354-5

1

A SMALL RAILWAY STATION on the line that leads to Russia.

For as far as the eye could see in both directions, four parallel tracks stretched into the distance along the yellowish gravel of the wide embankment; on the ground beside each line, like a dirty shadow, was a dark trace left by jets of burning-hot steam.

The wide road that led to the platform and the low, oil-painted station building was full of ruts. Its edges would have been indistinguishable from the trampled ground all around, had it not been for two rows of acacia trees that ran forlornly alongside, their parched leaves suffocating beneath layers of dust and soot.

Perhaps it was the dismal colours, or the pale, feeble light of the late-afternoon sun struggling to shine through the mist, but everything and everyone had something lacklustre, lifeless and mechanical about them, as if they had been transported here from a puppet theatre. At regular intervals the stationmaster came out of his office, and, his head always at the same angle, turned to look down the long stretch of track towards the little signal box, which was still not giving any indication of the approach of the express train that had been seriously delayed at the border; then with exactly the same movement of his arm he took out his pocket watch, shook his head and disappeared inside again, like one of the little figures on an old-fashioned clock tower which go in and out whenever it chimes the hour.

On a wide strip of beaten earth between the track and the station building, a collection of merry young people were milling excitedly around an older married couple who were at the centre of an animated conversation. Yet the cheerfulness of this group didn't appear genuine either; before it had carried even a short distance, their laughter seemed to die away and fall to the ground, as if it had run up against an invisible obstacle.

Frau Törless, the wife of Court Counsellor Törless – for this was the name of the woman of perhaps forty years old – hid her sad eyes, which were still red from weeping, behind a heavy veil. The moment had come to say goodbye. It was painful to have to let her only son go back and live among strangers for such a long time without being able to watch over and protect her little darling.

For the small town was in the eastern part of the Empire, far from the Imperial Capital, in an arid, agricultural region where few people lived.

The reason why Frau Törless was forced to suffer from knowing that her son was in such a distant and uninviting place was that in this town there was a famous military boarding school which had been built in the last century on land belonging to a religious order, no doubt in the hope that it would protect impressionable youth from the corrupting influence of the city.

This was where the sons of the country's best families were educated, after which they could enter the university, the army or the civil service, and whichever they chose – and the same applied to moving in the grandest social circles – there was no better recommendation than having been a pupil at W.

So, four years earlier, Törless's parents had given in to their boy's ambitious entreaties and arranged for him to attend this institution.

This decision had since been the cause of many tears. Hardly had the gates of the school closed irrevocably behind him than young Törless was seized by the most terrible and intense homesickness. Neither his lessons, nor the games on the large, lush playing fields in the grounds, nor any of the other activities that the boarding school provided succeeded in capturing his interest; he barely even took part. He seemed to see everything through a haze, and during the day he often found it difficult to fight back a desire to sob, while every night he cried himself to sleep.

He wrote home almost every day, lived only for these letters; everything else seemed unreal, trivial incidents, insignificant stages like the numerals on a clock face. But whenever he wrote he sensed he was in some way marked out, distinguished; something welled up inside him, like an island full of colour, miraculous suns shining in the midst of the sea of grey sensations that constantly surrounded him, hemming him in with its cold indifference. During the day, on the playing field or in the classroom, whenever he remembered that that evening he was going to write a letter it was as if he were wearing a golden key on an invisible chain round his neck, with which, when no one was looking, he could open the gate to a garden full of wonder.

The strange thing was that this sudden, overwhelming attachment to his parents came as something unexpected and slightly disconcerting. Far from having foreseen it, he had come to the school voluntarily and even gladly; in fact the first time he said goodbye to his mother he had laughed at her for not being able to hold back her tears. It was only after he had been alone for a few days, during which time he felt relatively happy, that it suddenly struck him with full force.

He told himself that it was simply homesickness, that he was missing his parents. In reality it was something more ill-defined and multifaceted. Because the "object" of this yearning, the photograph of his mother and father, played no part in it. By this

I mean the tangible, not quite present but nonetheless physical memory of a loved one which speaks to our every sense and is preserved by each of those senses, so that in everything we do we feel that person by our side, a silent, unseen presence. This soon dies away, like an overtone that vibrates barely longer than its fundamental note. For example, he could no longer conjure up the image of those who – at least to himself – he usually referred to as his "dearest darling parents". Whenever he tried, an endless agony would well up in him, a longing that tormented and yet perversely sustained him, because its searing flames brought both pain and rapture at once. As a result his parents were soon no more than a pretext for awakening this egotistical suffering, which imprisoned him in his voluptuous pride as if in a chapel, where, among hundreds of candles and the gaze of countless saints, incense floated above the agony of the flagellants.

As his "homesickness" became less intense and gradually faded, it still retained much of its distinct, particular character. Instead of bringing a sense of relief as he had expected, its going just left an empty space in young Törless's soul. And it was this void, this absence, that made him realize that it was not only a yearning that he had lost but something positive, an inner strength, something that had blossomed within him in the guise of suffering.

But now it was gone, and before he could become aware of the source of this, his first true feeling of happiness, it had had to run dry.

Around this time, the traces of fiery passion that his awakening soul had once left in his letters gave way to detailed descriptions of life at school and the new friends he was making.

As a result he felt impoverished and despoiled, like a young tree which after flowering in vain has to face its first winter.

His parents, however, were delighted. They loved him with a powerful, unthinking, animal affection. Every time he returned to school at the end of the holidays, to Frau Törless the house always seemed empty and lifeless, and for several days afterwards she would wander from room to room with tears in her eyes, occasionally caressing an object on which her child's eyes had rested or that his fingers had touched. For his sake, both she and his father would have let themselves be torn limb from limb.

The awkward emotions and passionate, defiant sadness of his letters caused them much pain and left them emotionally drawn; and so the serene, happy heedlessness that followed made them all the more glad and, believing that a crisis had been averted, they did their utmost to encourage him.

Assuming that suffering, like the healing process that followed, was a natural consequence of the current circumstances, neither of them recognized the symptoms of a specific psychological evolution. That it was the first, albeit unsuccessful attempt by a young person left to his own devices to develop his inner powers completely escaped them.

Törless was dissatisfied with life, and fumbled around in a vain attempt to find something new that might act as a foothold.

Around this time there was an episode that was indicative of the changes that were simmering inside him.

One day, young Prince H. arrived at the school. He came from one of the oldest, most influential and conservative families in the Empire.

The other boys found his gentle eyes soppy and affected; the way he had of swaying his hips as he stood up and fluttering his fingers when he spoke struck them as effeminate, and made them laugh. What amused them most of all, however, was that it was not his parents who had brought him to school, but his private tutor, who was a doctor of theology and a member of a religious order.

But from the outset he made a deep impression on Törless. Perhaps it was the fact that he was a prince who would one day be a member of the Court; whatever the case, this was a quite different breed of human being that he had discovered.

The Prince seemed to be infused with the tranquillity of old country houses and pious devotions. He walked with soft, graceful movements, in an almost timid way, as if trying to become smaller and less noticeable, a habit acquired from holding himself upright as he walked through a succession of large, empty rooms where all the other people seemed to be struggling with invisible obstacles.

Törless's acquaintanceship with the Prince was the source of a subtle psychological pleasure. It introduced him to the art of judging human nature, from which we learn to recognize a person by the timbre of their voice, the way they pick something up, even the tone of their silences, the manner in which their presence relates to the space around them; in short, that constantly changing, elusive and yet fundamental way of being a human being with a soul, which envelops all that is essential and tangible in the way flesh covers the skeleton, so that by coming to understand and appreciate the external we are able to discern the inner man.

For Törless this brief period was idyllic. He wasn't put off by his new friend's religious beliefs, although, as he was the product of a freethinking bourgeois family, they were unfamiliar to him. He accepted them without hesitation; in fact to him this was another of the Prince's merits, because they enhanced the singular nature of this person, who he sensed were completely different to himself, as well as being beyond compare.

When he was in the Prince's company he felt as if he had strayed into a chapel that stood a little way off the beaten track, yet the idea that he didn't really belong there disappeared into the sensual delight that came from suddenly seeing daylight through the chapel windows and letting his gaze run over the vain, gilt ornaments which had accumulated in the soul of this person, so much so that he could only see a confused image of it, as if his finger were unconsciously tracing the lines of a beautiful arabesque whose intertwinings followed the most bizarre rules.

Then suddenly they quarrelled and fell out.

Over a stupid thing, as Törless himself would later admit.

To be precise, they argued about religion. And from that moment on everything was over between them. As if deliberately disregarding his true feelings, Törless's reasoning mind launched a relentless assault on the Prince's sensibilities. He heaped his rational man's scorn on him, brutally tore down the filigree edifice in which his friend's soul felt at home, and the two of them parted company in a rage.

They never spoke to each other again. Törless was probably dimly aware that he had done something very foolish, and a hazy intuition told him that the crude, unbending criteria of intellect had, in the most untimely fashion, shattered something fine and precious. But there was nothing he could do about it. A form of nostalgia for what had gone before probably remained, yet it was as if he were caught up by a different current that was carrying him farther and farther away.

Not long afterwards the Prince left the school, where he had never really felt happy.

For Törless the world now consisted of boredom and emptiness. Yet he had grown, and the first obscure stirrings of adolescent sexuality were gradually awakening in him. At this stage he struck up a few friendships, of the type that suited someone of his age, and which later on were to be of great importance to him. Among them were Beineberg, Reiting, Moté and Hofmeier, the same boys who had been with him and his parents at the station.

Oddly enough they were the worst elements of his year, obviously from good families and no doubt gifted, but inclined to be unruly and boisterous to the point of cruelty. That Törless should have felt himself drawn to them in particular was probably due to a lack of self-confidence, which since his falling-out with the Prince had become more marked. In fact his choice of friends flowed directly from this estrangement, because, as that had been, it reflected a fear of finer feelings to which his new companions, with their rude health and heartiness, provided a powerful antidote.

Now at a certain stage in his intellectual development, he allowed himself to fall completely under their influence. At a school of this kind, a boy of his age has by now read Goethe, Schiller and Shakespeare, perhaps even a few modern authors. These are then regurgitated, half-digested, in various attempts at writing. From this emerge classical tragedies or sentimental verse clothed in page after page of rarefied language and syntax that resemble the finest lace. Such efforts may be ludicrous in themselves, yet they play an invaluable part in our inner evolution. Borrowed emotions or associations assimilated from external sources help a young person to find his way through the psychological quicksand of this time of life, when he longs to be someone but is not yet ready to take that step. Ultimately, it matters little if one individual retains something while another doesn't; each comes to terms with himself later in life, and so the risk only exists during this period of transition. If it were possible to make a young person see how ridiculous his character is the ground would open up beneath him, or he would collapse like a sleepwalker who suddenly wakes and sees nothing but a void.

Yet the art of illusion, that ploy which is of such benefit to human development, was something in which the school was not versed. On the shelves of its library there was no lack of classical literature, but this was regarded as dull, while the rest of the books were sentimental novellas or penny-dreadful war stories.

In his craving for literature, young Törless no doubt read every one of them, and a few trite, mawkish images might have made a passing impression on him, but none had what could be called a lasting influence on his character.

Yet at the time it didn't seem as if he had any character.

Every so often, for instance, influenced by books he had read, he would try his hand at writing a short story or a Romantic epic. Aroused by his heroes' unhappy love affairs his cheeks would blush scarlet, his pulse would race and his eyes would glaze over.

The moment he put the pen down, however, it was over; in a sense his mind only came alive when it was in a state of movement. Which is why he would have been able to dash off a poem or a short story, had he been asked to do so. He would set to with a will, although he never took it seriously: to him it didn't seem a worthwhile occupation. His personality contributed nothing to it, nor did it contribute anything to his personality. The only thing that could rouse him from his apathy and make him experience emotions was an external compulsion, in the way an actor has to have a part to play.

These were mental reactions. But at the time, what we experience as character or the soul, the outline or tonal colours of a human being – or at least those of them that show our thoughts, decisions and actions to be insignificant, incidental and interchangeable, such as what, outside of any intellectual considerations, had made him feel bound to the Prince – that ultimate and unchanging hinterland seemed to be something Törless didn't possess.

As for his friends, the delight they took in sport and life's more creaturely pleasures meant that they didn't feel the need for such things which are provided by a schoolboy's passing affair with literature.

But Törless was too intellectually inclined for the first of these, while in the case of the second, life at boarding school, which required everyone continually to defend his opinions, if necessary with his fists, had made him acutely sensitive to the ridicule that such second-hand emotions could attract. This bred a state of indecisiveness, an inner anguish that prevented him from discovering his true self.

He joined in with his new friends because their brutishness imposed itself on him. And, because he was ambitious, there were even times when he tried to outdo them. But he could never go the whole way, thus earning himself nothing but scorn. This left him all the more intimidated. During this critical period his whole existence was one constant attempt to emulate his boorish, virile friends, while deep down he was indifferent to these efforts.

Whenever his parents came to visit now, as long as he was alone with them he was shy and said little. Every time he found a different excuse to avoid his mother's affectionate embraces. If the truth were known he would have liked to return them, but felt ashamed, as if his classmates were watching.

His parents just took this as the awkwardness of adolescence.

In the afternoon the whole unruly gang appeared. They played cards, ate, drank, told jokes about the masters and smoked the cigarettes that Court Counsellor Törless had brought with him from the Imperial Capital.

Such high spirits delighted and reassured his parents.

They were unaware that for Törless there were times when things were very different here; and that recently these had become more frequent. At such moments, school life left him utterly indifferent. The cement that held his everyday cares and concerns together simply crumbled, and without this inner anchorage the different elements of his life fell apart.

Often he would sit for hours on end, lost in dark, gloomy thoughts, as if hunched over himself.

As on previous visits, his mother and father had stayed for two days. They had gone out for meals together, smoked, made a short local excursion; but now the express train was about to take his parents back to the capital.

A faint tremor in the line announced its approach, and to Frau Törless's ears the sound of the bell ringing on the station roof seemed as if it would never end.

"Well then, my dear Beineberg, you'll promise to keep an eye on my boy for me?" said Court Counsellor Törless, turning to young Baron Beineberg, a lanky, bony fellow with protruding ears, whose eyes were nonetheless expressive and intelligent.

Hearing himself treated as a child, Törless's face took on a disgruntled expression, while Beineberg gave a flattered and slightly gloating smirk that bore traces of malice.

"Actually," continued the Court Counsellor, turning to the others, "I might ask all of you to be so kind as to inform me straight away if anything should happen to my son."

Although he was used to being submitted to these displays of excessive concern every time they said goodbye, this last remark provoked an outburst of bored exasperation from Törless: "But Papa, whatever do you think could happen to me?"

Meanwhile the others clicked their heels, holding their elegant rapiers smartly to their sides, and the Court Counsellor added: "You never know what might happen, and the thought that I would be informed immediately is a source of great reassurance to me; after all, you may not be in a position to write yourself."

The train drew into the station. Court Counsellor Törless embraced his son, Frau von Törless drew her veil closer to her face to hide her tears, one after the other his friends expressed their thanks, and then the conductor closed the door of the carriage.

One last time Herr and Frau Törless looked at the tall, bleak rear façade of the main school building, the endless and imposing wall that surrounded the grounds, and then on either side only brownish-grey fields and the occasional fruit tree.

In the meantime the boys had left the station and, walking in single file in two ranks on either side of the road to avoid the worst and most persistent dust, made their way into the town, hardly saying a word to each other.

It was already past five o'clock, and the fields were taking on a chill and solemn appearance, as if heralding the approach of evening.

Törless suddenly felt very unhappy.

Perhaps it was because his parents had gone, or perhaps it was the dull, cheerless melancholy that hung over the surrounding countryside, blurring the outline of things only a short distance away with dark, lifeless colours.

The same terrible indifference that had weighed on the landscape all afternoon was now creeping across the plain, while the mist that followed behind it seemed to cling to the ploughed fields and leaden-coloured beet crops like a trail of mucus.

Without looking right or left, Törless could still feel it. One foot in front of the other he followed the path left in the dust by the boy ahead of him – and that was what he felt: that this was what he had to do, that a rigid, iron constraint was imprisoning him, forcing his whole life into this forward movement, step by step along this single straight line, along this narrow beaten track through the dust.

When they stopped at a crossroads where the road was joined by another at a small, circular patch of beaten earth, and a rotten wooden signpost sprung up lopsidedly, the contrast between this straight line and the surroundings was so strong that to him it had the effect of a cry of despair.

Then they set off again. He thought about his parents, about people he knew, about life. It was the time of day when one dressed for an evening reception or a trip to the theatre. Afterwards one went to a restaurant, listened to an orchestra, called in at the coffee house. One had an interesting encounter. An amorous adventure kept one's hopes up till daybreak. And life kept on turning like a miraculous fairground wheel, forever bringing something new, unexpected…

These thoughts made him sigh, and with every step that brought him closer to the restrictions of institutional life something deep down inside him knotted itself tighter and tighter together.

The bell was already ringing in his ears. There was nothing he feared quite as much as the sound of this bell, which announced the end of the day as if with a sharp, irrevocable blow of a knife.

No doubt his life would be uneventful, it would probably fade into the twilight of permanent apathy, but the ringing of this bell added its mocking voice to the emptiness, making him quiver with helpless rage at himself, at fate, at yet another day that was gone, dead and buried.

You're not permitted to live any more, for the next twelve hours you're not allowed to live, for the next twelve hours you're dead… that was what the bell was saying.

As the group of young men came to the first houses, which were low shacks, Törless's dark, brooding thoughts left him. As if his interest had suddenly been aroused he shot curious glances into the smoke-filled rooms of the grimy little buildings as they walked past.

On most of the doorsteps stood women wearing smocks and coarsely woven shirts, with large dirty feet and bare brown arms.

The younger, more strapping ones hurled vulgar witticisms in some Slavic dialect. They nudged each other and giggled at the "young gentlemen"; now and then one of them let out a shriek as her breasts were stroked rather too brazenly in passing, or responded to a slap on the thigh with a laugh and a curse. Many of them just watched with grave, angry expressions as the boys strode past; and if the peasant husband happened to appear he gave an awkward grin, half uneasy, half good-natured.

Törless didn't join in with his companions' displays of precocious masculinity.

This was no doubt due in part to the shyness in sexual matters that is characteristic of only children, but mostly to the particular nature of his sensuality, which was more covert, more powerful and of a darker complexion than that of his friends, less inclined to speak its name.

While the others treated the women with deliberate effrontery, probably more in an attempt to show form than out of actual desire, Törless was troubled and tormented by what was genuine shamelessness.

He threw such burning glances through the small windows and along the narrow, twisting passageways of the houses that it was as if a fine net were constantly dancing before his eyes.

Half-naked children were rolling around in the muck in the yards; now and then a woman's skirt rucked up as she was working, exposing her calves, or an ample bosom strained the seams of a bodice. And, as if all this were taking place in a quite different atmosphere, where an overpowering bestiality reigned, from the doors of the houses poured waves of stagnant air that Törless gulped down avidly.

It made him think of old paintings that he had seen in museums without really understanding them. He was waiting for something, just as he had stared at those paintings and waited for something, something that never happened. Such as... what? Something extraordinary and unheard of; an incredible sight that he couldn't begin to imagine; something of a sensual nature, terrifying and bestial, which would seize him in its claws, tear his eyes out, so to speak; an experience that in some as yet obscure way was connected with these women's grimy smocks, their rough hands, with... with him being defiled by the filth in the yards... No, no! And again all he could feel was the fiery net in front of his eyes; it couldn't be expressed in words, words made it seem more terrible than it really was; it was something mute, unspoken, a choking sensation in the throat, a passing thought, and only when it was put into words did it take shape; and even then it only bore a distant resemblance to it, like in an enormous enlargement in which not only can everything be seen in minute detail but also things that aren't there... which was still something to be ashamed of.

"Is the little boy homesick then?" von Reiting suddenly asked sarcastically. He was tall, two years older than Törless, and hadn't failed to notice his silence and sombre expression. Törless just gave a forced, self-conscious smile; it was as if the spiteful Reiting had read his mind.

He didn't reply. In the meantime they came to the church square of the little town, which was paved with cobblestones in the shape of cats' heads. Here they went their separate ways.

Törless and Beineberg didn't want to go back yet, but the others hadn't been given leave to be out after lock-up, and headed off towards the school.

2

THE TWO OF THEM went into the patisserie. They sat at a small, round table next to a window that looked onto the garden, beneath a gas lamp whose flame hissed faintly inside the opaque glass sphere of its shade.

They made themselves comfortable, drank one glass of schnapps after another and smoked, in between eating the occasional cake and savouring the pleasure of being the only customers, except for a solitary man sitting over a glass of wine in the far room. Apart from that everything was quiet; even the corpulent proprietor, a woman of a certain age, seemed to be asleep behind the counter.

His mind elsewhere, Törless gazed out of the window at the empty garden, where darkness was gradually falling.

Beineberg was talking. About India, as usual. His father, who was a general, had served there with the British Army. He had not only brought back small carved wooden objects, fabrics and mass-produced idols – as most Europeans did – but also something of the mysterious and fantastical shades of esoteric Buddhism. He had passed on what he had learnt, as well as what he had discovered from subsequent reading, to his son, although he was only a boy at the time.

He was a particular kind of reader. A cavalry officer and no great lover of books, he held literature and philosophy in equal contempt. If he did read, he didn't want to waste time pondering over opinions or academic debates: when he opened a book he expected it to be a gateway to higher wisdom. They had to be books the mere possession of which was the sign of belonging to a secret society, a guarantee of divine revelation. He only found this in the works of Hindu philosophy, which to him weren't simply books, but the revelations he sought; seminal works, like the alchemistic and magical writings of the Middle Ages.

It was with these that this hale and hearty man, scrupulous in the performance of his duties as well as riding all three of his horses almost every day, liked to shut himself away of an evening.

He would select a passage at random and reflect on it, in the hope that it might be that very night that it would reveal its innermost meaning to him. And never was he disappointed, although he was often forced to admit that he had yet to penetrate beyond the antechamber of the Temple.

So around this wiry, weather-beaten man hung a form of solemn secret. The belief that every evening he might find himself on the threshold of an earth-shattering discovery gave him an air of secretive superiority. Far from dreamy, his gaze was calm and steadfast. The habit of reading books where not a single word could be replaced without distorting the hidden meaning, the careful, respectful weighing-up of the primary and alternative meanings of every phrase, helped shape this expression.

From time to time, however, he would drift off into the half-light of blissful melancholia. This happened whenever his thoughts turned to the esoteric cult which was once bound to the original version of the texts he had in front of him, to the miracles they had inspired and the thousands of people who had been moved by them, thousands of people who, although separated from him by vast distances, seemed like his brothers, whereas those around him, whom he knew intimately, aroused nothing but his contempt. At moments like this he was disheartened. The thought that he was condemned to live out his life far from the source of these sacred energies, that his efforts might fail in the face of adverse circumstances, left him depressed. Yet if he sat over his books in this wretched state for a while, his mood would undergo a curious change. His wouldn't feel any less melancholy: quite the reverse, he would become more and more miserable, but it ceased to weigh on him. He no longer felt abandoned at his post, and yet within this nostalgia lay a subtle pleasure, the pride of doing something different, of serving a misunderstood deity. And for a fleeting moment something not unlike spiritual ecstasy would light up his eyes.

Beineberg talked himself hoarse. He was a larger, distorted version of his father, and had inherited all his traits; but what for the older man had perhaps at first been only a whim, maintained and refined purely for its outlandishness, in the son had developed into extravagant hopes. Each of his father's idiosyncrasies, which at heart might only have ever been the last refuge of individuality that everyone has to try to create – if only in the choice of clothes – in order to set oneself apart from other people, in him had become a firm belief that by means of exceptional psychological powers he would one day achieve a position of dominance.

Törless was all too familiar with this topic. It just washed over him.

He had half turned away from the window and was watching Beineberg roll a cigarette. Once again he felt the odd sense of revulsion for his friend that sometimes seized hold of him. The slender, dark-skinned hands that were slipping the tobacco into the paper so smoothly and carefully were actually quite beautiful. The slim fingers, the attractively domed, oval nails had a certain distinction. As did the dark-brown eyes, and the lean, lissom body. Admittedly his ears stuck out slightly, he had a small, irregularly shaped face and the proportions of his head were reminiscent of a bat. And yet when he compared these individual details, Törless had the distinct impression that they weren't flaws at all, but a perfect example of what made him feel so strangely unsettled.

A lean body – Beineberg's ideal was the steely-slim legs of the Homeric athletes – had a completely different effect on Törless. Up till now he had never attempted to account for this, and as he sat there no adequate comparison sprang to mind. He would have liked to look Beineberg in the eye, but his friend would have noticed, and he would have had to get involved in some discussion or other. But it was precisely because he was seeing him partly in the flesh and partly in his mind's eye that the difference occurred to him. If he tried to picture this body without clothes it was impossible to retain the image of unruffled slenderness, and instead saw restless, writhing movements, distorted limbs and crooked spines like those found in depictions of martyrs or the grotesque parades of fairground performers.

The hands, too, which he ought to have associated with elegant gestures, he could only imagine fidgeting and fumbling. And it was precisely these, Beineberg's best feature, which were the focus of his greatest revulsion. There was something obscene about them. Yes, that was the correct description. He also couldn't help finding something obscene in the disjointed movements that this body made. Yet in a sense it was in the hands that this sensation was concentrated, from where it transmitted a form of premonition of impending physical contact that made Törless's flesh creep. He found this notion astonishing and rather frightening. It was the second time that day that something to do with sex had, without warning and for no apparent reason, found its way into his thoughts.

Beineberg picked up a newspaper, and Törless was now able to study him more closely.

But when it came to it there was nothing to see that might even partly justify this unexpected association of ideas.

And yet despite the fact that his anxiety was unfounded, it only grew more intense. It was barely ten minutes since they had been sitting here in silence, and already he felt his revulsion reaching a peak. For the first time it seemed that a fundamental, defining mood might be appearing in his relationship with Beineberg; it was as if an ever-present, lively mistrust had suddenly risen to the surface of their consciousness.

The atmosphere became more and more strained. Törless longed to hurl insults at Beineberg, but couldn't find the right words. A kind of shame made him increasingly agitated, as if something had happened between them. Restlessly he began drumming his fingers on the table.

Eventually, in order to free himself from this peculiar condition, he turned and looked out of the window again.

Beineberg glanced up from his paper; then he read a few more lines, put it down and yawned.

No sooner was the silence broken than the pressure that Törless had been under was released. The moment was quickly submerged, washed away by trivia. It had been an alarm signal, now replaced by the same old indifference...

"How much longer have we got?" he asked.

"Two and a half hours."

Törless shrugged and then shuddered. Again he felt the cold, dead hand of imprisonment reaching out towards him. The timetable, the everyday relationships with his friends. Soon even his aversion for Beineberg, which for a moment had seemed to open up new horizons, would no longer exist.

"What's for supper?"

"I don't know."

"What's first period tomorrow?"

"Maths."

"Hm. Is there any prep to do?"

"A couple of new theorems in trigonometry; but you won't have any trouble, there's not much to them."

"And after that?"

"Divinity."

"Divinity? Oh yes, that's right. No doubt that'll be fun again! When I'm on form I think I could just as easily prove that two and two make five as I can that there's only One True God..."

Beineberg gave Törless a mocking look. "You amuse me when you say things like that; anyone would think it's a game for you; in fact I just saw a glint of enthusiasm in your eye..."

"And why not? Isn't it just glorious? There comes a point with all that business when you can't tell if people are lying, or if what they've made up is more real than the person who invented it."

"How so?"

"Obviously I don't mean it literally. Of course, we always know when someone is spinning a yarn; but there are times when it actually seems credible, and we stop dead in our tracks, as if mesmerized by our thoughts."

"Fine, but what do you find so amusing?"

"Just that. It's like a blow to the head, a fit of dizziness, a panic attack..."

"Come off it, that's nonsense."

"I wouldn't claim otherwise. But whatever the case, it's what I find most interesting about this school."

"So it's a form of mental gymnastics, but it doesn't lead anywhere."

"No," replied Törless, and turned and looked out at the garden again. Behind him – far, far behind – he could hear the hiss of the gas lamp. He was in pursuit of a feeling that had suddenly risen up in him like mournful mist.

"You're right. It doesn't lead anywhere. But we mustn't let ourselves believe that. Of all the things we do here every day, do any of them lead anywhere? What do we get out of it? I'm talking about something worth having, if you see what I mean. In the evening you know you've got through another day, that you've learnt this and that, kept to the timetable, but you still feel empty – inwardly, I mean: you have what might be described as an inner hunger..."

Beineberg muttered something about intellectual preparation, spiritual exercises, that they weren't ready to start yet, that that came later...

"Exercises? Preparation? For what? Do you know anything for certain? Perhaps you hope for something, but even that's vague. That's all it is: waiting eternally for something you know nothing about, except that you're waiting for it... It's so boring..."

"Boring..." Beineberg dragged out the word and shook his head.

Törless continued staring out at the garden. He thought he could hear dead leaves rustling in the wind. Then came that moment of utter silence which descends just before nightfall. For a few seconds the shapes that had been nestling deeper and deeper into the half-light, the colours that were dissolving, seemed to stand perfectly still, holding their breath...

"Have you ever noticed, Beineberg," said Törless, without turning round, "that at twilight there are moments quite unlike any other. Whenever I see them it brings back the same memory. Of when I was very young, and I was playing in the woods. My nursemaid had wandered off; I didn't notice and thought I could still feel her nearby. Then all of a sudden something made me look up. I sensed that I was alone. It had gone terribly quiet. And as I looked round I got the impression that the trees were standing in a circle round me, silently watching me. I began to cry; I felt that the grown-ups had abandoned me, left me to the mercy of inanimate creatures... What is that feeling? I often have it even now. That sudden silence, like a language that we can't quite understand?"

"I don't know what you mean; but why shouldn't things have a language of their own? We can't even say with certainty that they don't have a soul!"

Törless didn't answer. He didn't think much of Beineberg's theories.

After a while his friend added: "Why do you keep looking out of the window? What's there to see?"

"I'm still wondering what it might be."

The fact was that his thoughts had moved on much further than he cared to admit. The state of extreme tension, of constantly keeping his ear to the ground to hear some vital secret, the effort of trying to discover an as yet uncharted aspect of life was something he had only been able to endure for a few minutes. And then he was engulfed by the feeling of isolation and abandonment that always followed whenever he demanded too much of himself. He sensed that there was something about this experience that was still too difficult for him, so his thoughts sought sanctuary in another part of it which in a sense hovered in the background, lying in wait: solitude.

Out in the deserted garden, a leaf sometimes danced in the light from the window, and a pale streak on the underside would glint as it tumbled back into the darkness, which seemed to give way, retreat, and then advance again until it stood motionless outside the window like a wall. This darkness was a world within a world. Like a black-clad enemy horde it swept across the earth, killing human beings or driving them away, obliterating all trace of their existence.

Törless got a sense of enjoyment from this idea. At this particular moment he didn't like human beings, grown-ups, adults. He never liked them at night. It was a time of day when he preferred to put them out of his mind. The world took on the appearance of a dark, empty house, and his heart contracted at the thought that he might have to search the rooms one by one – rooms full of shadows, where he didn't know what the corners concealed – tiptoeing through doorways that human feet would never pass through again, until he reached a room where the doors suddenly closed behind and in front of him, and he was face to face with the queen of the black-clad host. And then all the other doors slammed shut as well and, stretching into the distance beyond the walls, there was only darkness and its shadows, standing guard like black-robed eunuchs to keep everyone at bay.

Ever since the day he had been abandoned in the woods to cry, this had been his own particular solitude. For him it had all the attractions of a woman, and also something terrible and inhuman. He could sense the female presence, but her breath made him feel as if he were being strangled, her face was a swirling eddy into which all other human faces disappeared, while the movements of her hands were shudders running through his body.

He was afraid of these imaginings, because he was conscious of the secret depravity they concealed, and the thought that such images might gain control over him was extremely unsettling. But just when he felt that he was at his most serious and pure, they chose that moment to assail him. It may have been a reaction to the times when he sensed he was about to make some highly sensitive discoveries, which, even if they were already fermenting inside him were quite advanced for someone his age. Early in the development of any finely tuned moral powers there comes a point where the soul is weakened by something that might one day become its most audacious experience, as if its roots need to find their way down and churn up the ground that they will later hold together – which is why young people with a promising future generally have a past filled with humiliations.

Törless's preference for certain moods was the first sign of a psychological development that would later manifest itself as a gift for amazement. It was a curious ability that in time would come to rule his life. He would often be unable to prevent himself from experiencing events, people, things and even himself in a way that he felt was both incomprehensible and yet evidence of an affinity which could neither be explained nor wholly justified. They seemed to have palpable meaning, and yet they couldn't be fully translated into words and thoughts. Between events and his actual self, even between his emotions and a deeper, inner self about which he longed to know more lay a dividing line which, like the horizon, retreated from his desires the more he approached it. The closer his thoughts came to grasping his feelings, the more familiar and at the same time more bizarre and impenetrable they became, so that it no longer seemed as if they were moving away from him, but that it was he who was drifting away from them, although he could never quite dispel the illusion that he was getting closer.

Later on this extraordinary, almost unfathomable contradiction would account for a lengthy phase in his intellectual development, and seemed as if it would almost tear his soul apart, threatening to become his most serious problem.

For the time being, however, the intensity of the struggle was only apparent in the sudden but not infrequent bouts of listlessness that preceded it, frightening him from a distance, so to speak, whenever a strange, ambiguous mood gave him prior warning, as had happened a few moments ago. At times like this he would feel as powerless as a convict or a prisoner of war, as isolated from himself as he was from everyone else; he would have liked to cry out in despair at this emptiness, but instead he turned away from the solemn, ever-hopeful, tormented and lethargic human being inside him and – still terrified by this sudden renouncement but in raptures at its warm, guilty breath – listened for the whispering voice of solitude.

Suddenly he suggested they pay the bill. Beineberg's eyes gave a flicker of comprehension – it was a mood he knew of old. Törless loathed this complicity; it rekindled his aversion for Beineberg, and he felt defiled by the mere fact of associating with him.

But the two things went almost hand in hand. Defilement is just another form of solitude, one more wall of darkness.

Without saying a word they set off in a familiar direction.

3

I T MUST HAVE BEEN raining slightly, because the air was still damp and heavy. An opalescent mist quivered round the streetlamps, while here and there the paving stones shimmered.

Törless's sword kept catching on the cobbles, and he held it close to his side, but the sound of his heels clacking was enough to send a shudder down his spine.

It wasn't long before the ground under their feet became softer, they left the town centre behind and made their way along wide village streets towards the river.

The black water wound idly by, making hollow lapping noises as it flowed under the wooden bridge. Beside it stood a lone streetlamp, its glass smashed and dusty. Buffeted by gusts of wind, the beam of light lit up the occasional swirling wave before melting away on the crest. As they walked across, the round poles shifted beneath them, rolled back and forth...

Beineberg stopped. The opposite bank was lined with bushy trees, and like the road that ran at right angles to the bridge, it followed beside the river like a dark, threatening, impenetrable wall. Only after a search did they find the narrow, hidden path that led straight on. Whenever their uniforms brushed the dense undergrowth they were showered with raindrops. After a while they stopped and lit a match. It was now totally silent, they couldn't even hear the babble of the river. Then from somewhere in the distance came a confused, muffled noise. It might have been a scream or a warning; or just the call of some unintelligible creature that was finding its way through the bushes, much the same as they were. They strode in the direction of the sound, paused, and then carried on. After a quarter of an hour at most, with sighs of relief they made out raucous voices and the sound of an accordion.

The trees were sparser now, and they soon came to the edge of a clearing in the centre of which stood a substantial, two-storeyed square building.

It was the old public baths. There was a time when the local farmers and people from the town had made use of it, but it had stood virtually empty for years. Now a bar of ill repute had taken over the ground floor.

For a moment they stood quietly, listening.

Just as Törless was about to step out of the bushes, the sound of heavy boots rasped on the floorboards in the hall, and a drunk came lurching into view. Behind him in the half-darkened corridor was a woman; they could hear her muttering in a sharp, angry voice, as if demanding something. The man just laughed and swayed back and forth. Then there was what sounded like pleading, but it wasn't any more intelligible. The only thing that was unmistakable was her cajoling tone. Then the woman came outside and put her hand on the man's shoulder. Immediately she was lit up by the moonlight – her petticoat, her jacket, her imploring smile. The man stared straight ahead, shook his head and kept his hands thrust deep in his pockets. Then he spat and pushed the woman away. She had probably said something. The voices were louder now, and they could understand what was being said.

"So you aren't going to pay? Now listen here…"

"Why don't you go back upstairs, slut!"

"What! You peasant lout!"

By way of answer the drunk crouched down awkwardly and picked up a stone. "If you don't clear off sharpish I'll beat your brains out, you idiot!" Törless heard the woman rush up the stairs with a parting curse.

For a moment the man stood deliberating, the stone still in his hand. He laughed and looked up at the sky, where a yellow moon scudded between dark clouds; then he turned and stared at the undergrowth, as if trying to decide which way to go. His heart in his mouth, Törless gingerly moved his foot back. Eventually the drunk seemed to make up his mind. He dropped the stone and, with a coarse, triumphant laugh, hurled an obscenity up at the window and disappeared round the corner.

The two of them didn't move.

"Did you see who it was?" whispered Beineberg. "It was Božena."

Törless didn't reply; he was listening in case the drunk came back. Then suddenly Beineberg pushed him from behind. With a few swift, cautious strides, skirting round the wedge-shaped shafts of light from the ground-floor windows, they were in the dark hallway. A narrow wooden staircase wound sharply up to the floor above. Their footsteps must have made the stairs creak, or a sword clattered against the banisters, because the door of the bar opened and someone came to see who was there, while the accordion stopped playing and the babble of voices died away for a second or two.

Alarmed, Törless shrunk back against the wall. Despite the darkness they seemed to have seen him, because as the door closed he heard the barmaid's sarcastic voice, followed by roars of laughter.

On the upstairs landing it was pitch black. They hardly dared put one foot in front of the other for fear of knocking something over and making a noise. Eagerly, excitedly, they groped for the door handle.

Božena was a country girl who had moved to the city, where she went into service and eventually became a chambermaid.

At first everything went well. Her simple, peasant manner and firm, lumbering gait earned the trust of her mistresses, who appreciated her unspoilt nature with its whiff of the cowshed, as well as the love of her masters, who had a taste for its bouquet. Then, possibly on a whim, perhaps out of dissatisfaction and an unspoken yearning to live life to the full, she gave up this comfortable existence. She became a barmaid, was taken ill, found work in a high-class brothel, and gradually, increasingly eaten up by her dissolute way of life, she was washed up in a series of provincial backwaters, each more isolated than the last.

And it was here, not far from the village where she was born, that she had ended up living for the last few years, helping out in the bar during the day and spending her evenings smoking, reading cheap novels and entertaining the occasional man.

She hadn't quite become ugly yet, although her features were conspicuously lacking in charm, something she seemed to go out of her way to draw attention to with her behaviour. She was fond of letting it be known that she was conversant with the life of refinement and the ways of high society, but that she was now above such things. Rarely did she miss an opportunity to tell people that she couldn't give a damn about herself or anything else. Despite her fall from grace this earned her a certain esteem among the local peasant lads. Even if they spat at the mention of her name, and felt obliged to behave more uncouthly to her than to other young women, deep down they were enormously proud of this "lost soul" who was one of their own, and who had caught a glimpse of the world beneath the varnish. Alone and no doubt surreptitiously they always came back to have a good time with her. In this way she enjoyed a few last crumbs of pride and self-worth. Yet she derived what was perhaps even greater satisfaction from her dealings with the young gentlemen from the military boarding school. For them she made a point of displaying her coarsest, most unattractive qualities, because – as she was in the habit of saying – it didn't stop them from coming crawling back to her when they felt the need.

When the two friends walked in she was lying on the bed, smoking and reading as usual.

Standing in the doorway, Törless took in the sight with greedy eyes.

"My God, what a pair of nice boys!" she exclaimed sarcastically, looking them up and down disparagingly as they came in. "Really, Herr Baron! What would Mama say?"

This was her usual opening gambit.

"Give it a rest!…" muttered Beineberg, sitting down on the bed beside her. Törless sat farther away; he was piqued that she hadn't taken any notice of him and was behaving as if she didn't recognize him.

Of late his visits to this woman had become his sole, secret delight. By the end of the week he was becoming restless and could hardly wait for Sunday, when he would slip out to see her. More than anything else it was this need for clandestine behaviour that constantly preoccupied him. But what if a group of drunks, such as the ones in the bar a few minutes ago, took it into their heads to come after him – just for the pleasure of giving the depraved young toff a thrashing? He was no coward, but he knew he was totally defenceless here. Compared with their big rough fists, his dainty little sword was ridiculous. And then there was the disgrace and punishment that would follow! He would have little choice but to run away or resort to begging. Or get Božena to protect him. He shuddered at the very thought. But that was all it was, nothing else! It was this same fear that always attracted him, the surrender of self. Giving up his privileged position, mixing with the common people; being below them – less than them!

He wasn't depraved. When it came to the act itself, his revulsion for it and its possible consequences always prevailed. His imagination had simply taken an unhealthy turn. Whenever the weekday routine weighed on him like lead, these corrosive attractions would begin to beckon. The memory of his visits developed into a unique form of temptation. He saw Božena as the casualty of a monstrous process of decline, and his relationship with her, the emotions he experienced, as a ritual of self-sacrifice. What fascinated him was being forced to abandon the things that imprisoned him, his privileged position, the ideas and feelings with which he was constantly inoculated, everything that stifled him while offering nothing in return. What fascinated him was the thought of running naked, divested of everything, escaping to seek sanctuary with this female.

In this he was little different from most adolescents. If Božena had been pure and lovely and he thus had been able to fall in love with her, he might have bitten into her, raised both his and her sensual desires to the lofty heights of pain. Because a young adult's first great passion is never love for an individual, but hatred of everyone. The feeling of being misunderstood by and not understanding the world around us, far from being attendant on our first passion, is its sole, essential cause. And this passion is itself an escape, where being two only brings redoubled solitude.

The first passion rarely lasts, and leaves a bitter taste. It is a mistake, a disappointment. Afterwards we no longer understand who we are, don't know at whose feet to lay the blame. For the most part it is because the actors in this drama only know each other by coincidence: they are chance companions, both trying to escape. No sooner has the agitation left them than they no longer recognize each other. They only see what divides them, because they no longer see what they have in common.

The only difference with Törless was that he was alone. The dissipated and ageing prostitute wasn't capable of releasing the forces that lay deep within him. Yet she was enough of a woman to take those elements of his inner life, which like seeds were waiting for the moment of fertilization, and in a sense drag them to the surface prematurely.

These, then, were his peculiar ideas, the temptations of his imagination. Yet there were times when he felt like throwing himself to the ground and crying out in despair.

Božena still wasn't taking any notice of Törless. It seemed as if she were doing it out of spite, to annoy him. Then suddenly she broke off the conversation: "Give me some money and I'll go and get some tea and schnapps."

Törless handed her one of the silver coins that his mother had given him that afternoon.

She took a battered spirit burner from the window sill, lit it, then shuffled down the stairs.

Beineberg gave Törless a prod. "Why are you being so wet? She'll think you're in a funk."

"Leave me out of it," replied Törless. "I'm not in the mood. Just talk to her by yourself. And why does she always go on about your mother, by the way?"

"Ever since she found out my name she's been saying that she used to work for my aunt, which is where she met my mother. There may be a grain of truth in it, but she's making a lot of things up – just for the fun of it; although I don't see what's so amusing."

Törless blushed; he had just had an odd thought. But then Božena reappeared with the schnapps, sat next to Beineberg on the bed again and picked up the conversation where she had left off.

"…Oh yes, your Mama was a beautiful girl. You don't look much like her with those protruding ears of yours. And she was fun-loving with it. I bet she turned more than a few men's heads. Good for her."

There was a pause, and then she seemed to remember something particularly amusing: "Do you remember your uncle, the one who was an officer in the Dragoons? I think his name was Karl, he was your mother's cousin – and he paid court to her in those days, didn't he just! But on Sundays when the ladies were in church he used to come chasing after me. Every five minutes I had to be taking this, that or the other up to his room. He was a fine-looking fellow, I can tell you, not the sort to be backward about coming forward…" She gave a knowing laugh. And she began to elaborate on the subject, which was clearly a source of special pleasure for her. She spoke in a familiar way, and her words seemed deliberately designed to tarnish everyone involved. "…What I mean to say is, I think your mother took a shine to him too. If only she'd known… I think your aunt would have had no choice but to chuck the pair of us out, him and me! But that's fine ladies for you, 'specially when they don't have a man of their own. Dear Božena this, dear Božena that – that was how it was from dawn till dusk! But when the cook got herself in the family way, well, there was a real to-do! I'm sure they thought the likes of us only washed our feet once a year. They didn't say nothing to the cook, mind, but when I was working in the next room I heard them talking about her. From the expression on your mother's face you'd have thought butter wouldn't melt in her mouth! Of course, it wasn't long before your aunt had a bun in the oven too…"

As she was speaking, Törless felt unable to resist her vulgar innuendos.

It was as if he could see what she was describing right in front of his eyes. Beineberg's mother was transformed into his own. He remembered the light, airy rooms of the family apartment. The clean, well-groomed, unapproachable faces that inspired a certain respect in him during dinner parties at home. The cold, distinguished hands that never seemed to stoop to anything so degrading as eating. A host of details came flooding back to him, and he felt ashamed to be in this fetid little room, trembling to find a response to humiliating remarks made by a whore. The memory of the exquisite manners of a society where good form was always maintained had a more powerful influence on him than any moral considerations. The obscure morass of his passions suddenly struck him as absurd. With the intensity of a vision he saw the scandalized smile, the coolly dismissive wave of the hand with which he would be ejected like a grubby little animal. Yet he didn't move, as if he were tied to the chair.

With every detail he remembered, along with the shame came a growing collection of base thoughts. The first of these had appeared while Beineberg was explaining what Božena had said, which was why he had blushed.

At the time he had been unable to stop himself thinking of his own mother, and this thought now had such a hold on him that he couldn't shake it off. At first it only touched the outer limits of his consciousness, too much like a flash of lightning or something glimpsed in the distance to be described as a thought. And then in quick succession came a series of questions whose purpose was to block this out: "How can it be that this Božena creature is able to make a connection between her unsavoury existence and my mother's? That she coexists with her within the confines of the same thought? Why doesn't

she touch the ground with her forehead before she mentions
her name? Why isn't it clear from what she's saying that they
have nothing in common, that there's a gulf between them?
How can this be? For me this woman is just a mass of sexual
desires; while up till now my mother has floated far above my
life like a heavenly body beyond all earthly longings, existing
in a pure, blue, unclouded and infinite sky…"

Yet none of these questions was the most important one; in
fact they hardly had any effect on him. They were only secondary, something that occurred after the event. If they echoed each
other it was because none of them got to the heart of the matter.
They were merely excuses, paraphrases, a means of disguising
the fact that, quite suddenly, instinctively and premeditatedly,
he had experienced a concatenation of emotions that answered
these questions before they had been asked, but in the wrong
way. He feasted his eyes on Božena while unable to stop thinking about his mother, and thus a connection was established
between the two women; everything else was just a desperate
attempt to wriggle his way out of this tangle of ideas. This
was the only true fact. But the futility of his efforts to shake
off this yoke took on an obscure and terrifying significance
that dogged him like a duplicitous smile.

In order to chase these thoughts from his mind, Törless looked
around the room. But by now they had left their imprint on
everything: the cast-iron stove with a rusty top, the bed with
its rickety legs and peeling, painted headboard, the holes
in the bedspread through which the dirty sheets were visible; Božena herself, her chemise, with one of its straps half
hanging off her shoulder, her cheap, rose-coloured petticoat,
her loud, chattering laugh; and then there was Beineberg,
whose behaviour reminded him of a licentious priest gone
mad who was interspersing the solemnity of a prayer with

double entendres… everything was heading in one direction, constantly besieging him, compelling his thoughts to follow the same road.

Shifting from one object to another, his anxious gaze could find solace in only one place: the gap above the curtains at the window. From there he could see the clouds in the sky, the still, silent moon.

It was like walking out into the cool, tranquil night air. For a moment his mind stopped turning. And then a pleasant memory came back to him. The house in the country where they had spent the summer. Nights in the silent grounds. The dark-blue-velvet heavens filled with trembling stars. His mother's voice coming from the depths of the garden, where she was walking with Papa on the shimmering gravel paths. The songs that she sang softly to herself. But then… and a shudder ran through him… he felt the same agonizing comparisons. What did the two of them feel when they were alone together? Love? It had never occurred to him before. No, love was something completely different. Not something for grown-up people; still less for his parents. To sit by an open window at night and feel abandoned, to feel different from adults, to be misunderstood by every laugh and mocking glance, never able to explain who you really were, to yearn for someone who would understand… that was love! But for that you had to be young and alone. It was different for older people, surely; something calm and composed. Mama just sang in the garden in the darkness of evening and was cheerful…

But this was precisely what Törless couldn't understand. He didn't realize that the patient plans which for adults bind the days, months and years together were still unknown to him. Like the dulling of the senses that stops us worrying that yet another day has come to an end. His life was focused on individual days. For him, each night was oblivion, obliteration, a tomb. He had yet to learn to lie down to die at night without letting it worry him.

As a result he assumed that something lay behind this, something that people were concealing from him. For him the night was a dark gateway leading to mysterious pleasures to which he hadn't been given the key, and so his life remained empty and unhappy.

He remembered noticing how his mother had laughed in an unusual way on one of those evenings, how she squeezed her husband's arm more tightly and playfully. It seemed to rule out any doubt. There had to be another door, one that led out of the world inhabited by these serene and hallowed beings. And now he knew this, he couldn't think about it without giving the knowing smile with which he tried vainly to defend himself from malign suspicions…

In the meantime Božena was still talking. Törless was only half listening. She mentioned someone else who also came to see her nearly every Sunday… "What's his name now? He's in your year."

"Reiting?"

"No."

"What does he look like?"

"About as tall as him." Božena gestured towards Törless. "Except his head's bigger."

"What, Basini?"

"Yes, that's the one. He's rather comical. And posh; he only drinks wine. But he's stupid. It costs him a small fortune, but all he ever does is talk. He never stops bragging about the so-called affairs he's had back home; but what did he do exactly? It's obvious he's never been with a woman. I mean, you're just a schoolboy too, but you know what's what; he's all fingers and thumbs and scared stiff: that's why he goes on about how a bon vivant – yes, that's the expression he used! – is supposed to handle a woman. He says women aren't fit for anything else – where does one of you get that sort of thing from, that's what I'd like to know!"

Beineberg just sniggered sarcastically.

"You can laugh as much as you like!" Božena retorted, clearly amused. "I asked him once if he wouldn't be ashamed to talk like that in front of his mother. 'Mother?...' he replies. 'Mother? Who's that? She doesn't exist any more. I left all that behind when I came here...' Oh yes, prick up those big ears of yours why don't you, but that's what you lot are like! Nice sons you are, fine young gentlemen! It's me your mothers ought to feel sorry for!..."

Hearing this, Törless saw himself as he had earlier. Leaving everything behind, breaking away from his parents' image. But now he was confronted with the fact that what he was doing was nothing terrible: in fact it was utterly mundane. He felt ashamed. Yet the other thoughts hadn't left him. They're doing the same thing! They're betraying you! You have hidden accomplices! Maybe it's slightly different for them, although it must be almost the same as it is for you: a terrible, secret pleasure. Somewhere you can drown yourself and your fear of everyday monotony... Perhaps they knew more than he did... something absolutely extraordinary? Because during the day they were so calm and unruffled... and that laugh of his mother's?... as if she were going quietly from room to room, closing all the doors...

There came a point in this inner conflict where, sick at heart, Törless gave himself up to the storm.

It was at this moment that Božena came over to him.

"Why isn't the young 'un saying anything? Is there something wrong?"

Beineberg gave a malicious grin and whispered in her ear.

"Homesick, eh? Has Mama gone and left him? And the first thing the horrid little boy does is come running to someone like me!"

With feigned tenderness she ran her fingers through Törless's hair. "Come on, don't be silly. Give us a kiss. Even you posh types won't break if I touch you." And she tilted his head back.

Törless wanted to reply, to pull himself together and produce some uncouth witticism; he sensed that the most important thing was to say something, it didn't matter what, but he didn't utter a sound. With a fixed smile he just stared at the face above him, into the unseeing eyes, and then the world around him began to shrink… to drift farther and farther away… the image of the young peasant with the stone flashed through his mind, as if jeering at him… and then he was completely alone…

4

"GUESS WHAT," whispered Reiting, "I've got him."
"Who?"
"The locker thief."

Törless and Beineberg had just got back. It was almost supper time, and the duty prefect had gone. Various groups were standing around chatting among the green tables, the room was a hive of activity.

It was the standard schoolroom, with whitewashed walls, a large black crucifix and portraits of the Emperor and Empress either side of the blackboard. Beside the tall cast-iron stove, which hadn't been lit yet, the boys who had been at the station with Törless and his parents that afternoon were sitting on the dais or on upturned chairs. As well as Reiting there was Hofmeier, who was very tall, and a little Polish count who was always known as Dschjusch.

Törless's curiosity was immediately aroused.

The lockers were at the back of the classroom. They consisted of long chests divided into compartments in which pupils kept books, letters, money and every imaginable kind of trinket.

For some time boys had been complaining that small amounts of money were going missing, although none of them had any definite theories as to the culprit.

Beineberg was the first to be able to say with certainty that he had had a more substantial sum stolen the previous week. But only Reiting and Törless knew about this. They suspected the school servants.

"So who is it?" said Törless.

Reiting put his finger to his lips. "Ssh! Later. No one else knows yet."

"Is it one of the servants?" whispered Törless.

"No."

"At least give me a clue."

Moving away from the others, Reiting lowered his voice and said, "B." Apart from Törless no one would have understood a word of this guarded conversation. But he was staggered by this information. B.? It could only mean Basini. And that was impossible! His mother was extremely wealthy, his guardian was an "Excellency". Törless couldn't believe it, but then what Božena had said suddenly came back to him.

He could hardly wait for everyone else to go in to supper. Beineberg and Reiting didn't join them, making the excuse that they had had too much to eat that afternoon.

Reiting suggested that before doing anything else it would be best if they went "upstairs".

They set off along the long corridor that led from the schoolroom. The flickering gas lamps cast very little light, and they walked so quietly that the sound of their footsteps only carried from one alcove to the next.

After about fifty metres they came to a staircase that led up to the second floor, which housed the natural-history department, various other collections and a number of disused classrooms.

From here on the stairs became narrower, leading to the attic in a series of sharp, right-angled stages. As older buildings were often constructed in defiance of logic, with many unnecessary nooks and crannies and redundant steps, they climbed considerably higher than the level of the attic, and to reach the locked, heavy iron door that led to it they had to go down yet another flight of wooden stairs.

At this point they found themselves in a large, empty space, several metres high and reaching all the way up to the rafters. It was probably a place where no one came any more, and was used to store scenery from long-forgotten school plays.

Even during the day the staircase was always shrouded in a half-light of ancient dust, since, being in a remote wing of the massive school building, it was rarely used.

When they reached the last flight of stairs, Beineberg vaulted over the bannisters, and then, holding on to the bars, slipped down between the pieces of scenery, followed by Reiting and Törless. Finding a foothold on a crate that was put there for the purpose, with a final leap they landed on the floor.

If someone standing on the staircase had looked in this direction, even once their eyes grew accustomed to the dark it would still have been impossible to make out anything more than a jagged mass of scenery flats crammed against each other.

As Beineberg moved one of these aside, a narrow passageway appeared.

They hid the crate that they had used to climb down on, and squeezed between the scenery.

It was pitch dark, and finding their way required an intimate knowledge of the place. A tall canvas panel would sometimes rustle as one of them brushed against it, and dust cascaded onto the floorboards, scattering like a horde of startled mice and bringing with it the smell of musty packing cases. The three friends, who were familiar with the route, groped their way forward step by step, so as not to snag one of the pieces of string that they had stretched just above floor level to act as tripwires and alarm signals.

It took quite a while for them to reach a small door on the right-hand side, next to the outer wall of the attic.

When Beineberg opened it they found themselves in a cramped space below the last flight of stairs, which, in the flickering light from an oil lamp that Beineberg lit, took on a fantastical appearance.

The only part of the ceiling that was horizontal was the area directly below the little landing, and even there it was only just high enough for someone to stand upright. It then sloped down towards the back, following the line of the staircase and finishing in a sharp angle. At the opposite, gable end was the partition that separated the attic from the stairs, while the longer wall was provided by the stonework that supported the staircase. Only the second lateral wall, where the door was, seemed to have been built specifically. It probably owed its existence to a need for storage space, or the whim of the architect, who when he saw this dark corner came up with the medieval idea of turning it into a hiding place.

Whatever the case, the three friends were probably the only people in the school to know of its existence, let alone think of using it for this purpose.

So when it came to furnishings, they had been able to indulge their taste for the bizarre.

The walls were covered with blood-red bunting that Reiting and Beineberg had purloined from one of the attic rooms, and the floor with two layers of the heavy woollen blankets that were used as extra bedding in the dormitories during winter. At the front were three small, low chests covered in fabric, which served as seats; at the far end, in the corner where the sloping ceiling met the floor, they had set up a place to sleep.

It was big enough for three or four people, shut off from the light and the rest of the room by a curtain.

On the wall beside the door hung a loaded revolver.

Törless didn't like this room. The fact that it was small and isolated doubtless appealed to him: it was like being deep inside a mountain, and the smell of dusty scenery filled him with all manner of vague, confusing sensations. But the idea of a secret hiding place, tripwires, the revolver, all of which were supposed to heighten the illusion of clandestine revolt, struck him as ridiculous. It was as if they were desperate to convince themselves that they were a band of brigands.

If Törless played along, it was only because he didn't want to be left out. Beineberg and Reiting, on the other hand, took it all terribly seriously. Törless was aware of this. He also knew that Beineberg had duplicate keys to all the cellar and attic rooms in the school, and would often disappear from class for several hours and go somewhere or other – either to the uppermost rafters in the roof, or underground into one of the warrens of dilapidated vaults – where he would sit and read adventure stories or meditate on the supernatural by the light of a small lamp that he always took with him.

He knew similar things about Reiting, who had his own hiding places, where he kept his secret diaries. These were filled with daring plans for the future, as well as detailed records of the causes, management and progress of the countless intrigues that he incited among his classmates. For Reiting there was no greater pleasure than stirring up ill feeling among people, using one boy to bring about the downfall of another and revelling in the favours and fawning remarks that he extorted from them, and behind which he could sense the antipathy of hatred.

"I'm just practising" was the only explanation he ever gave, invariably with a charming smile. It was probably also to "practise" that on most days he would take himself off to some remote spot and box against a wall, a tree or a table to strengthen his arms and get calluses on his hands.

Törless knew about all of this, although he only understood it up to a point. Once or twice he had gone along with Reiting and Beineberg. The unconventional nature of their pursuits appealed to him – and he also enjoyed coming back into the daylight afterwards, into the midst of cheerful classmates, while still being able to feel the excitement of solitude and the delirium of darkness quivering in his eyes and ears. But if Beineberg or Reiting used these occasions as an opportunity to talk to someone else about themselves, to set out their ideas and explain what motivated them, then what they said completely escaped him. In fact he thought Reiting was slightly neurotic. His friend was fond of telling people that his father, who had always been an odd, unstable individual, had suddenly disappeared one day without leaving a trace. His name was probably assumed in order to conceal a grand aristocratic lineage. He was waiting for his mother to initiate him into the secret of his considerable birthright, envisaged a future of *coups d'état* and high politics, and wanted to be an officer.

For Törless it was impossible even to conceive of such ambitions. As far as he was concerned the age of revolutions was over. And yet Reiting's intentions were deadly serious – albeit on a small scale at this stage. He was a true tyrant, merciless to anyone who opposed him. His followers changed on a daily basis, but he always commanded the support of the majority. This was his greatest talent. A year or two earlier he had declared war on Beineberg, a conflict that had resulted in the latter's defeat. In the end Beineberg found himself almost totally isolated, although when it came to character assessment, cold-bloodedness and the ability to incite animosity against those he disliked he had little to envy his opponent. But he lacked Reiting's charm and powers of persuasion. His phleg-matic nature and unctuous philosophizing invariably aroused suspicions. People sensed that in the depths of his being he was capable of the most appalling excesses. Nonetheless he managed to make life difficult for Reiting, whose victory was eventually little more than a matter of chance. Ever since then they had deemed it best to combine forces.

All this left Törless indifferent. In any case, he didn't possess the necessary expertise for it. Yet he was still a prisoner in this world, witnessed with his own eyes every day what it meant to occupy the highest position in an empire – for in a school of this kind, every class is an empire in miniature. So he had a wary respect for his two friends. The occasional vague impulses that he felt to try to rival them went no further than amateurish attempts. As a result, and also being the youngest, his relationship with them was one of disciple or assistant. He benefitted from their protection, yet they gladly listened to his advice. Because of the three of them Törless had the most agile mind. Once on the right track he was capable of devising far and away the subtlest, most fertile twists and turns of reasoning. When it came to predicting what a particular individual could be expected to do in a particular set of circumstances, he was unequalled. But if it involved making a decision, taking a risk and acting on one of the psychological possibilities then he would shy away, lose all interest and enthusiasm. Nonetheless, it amused him to play the secret chief of staff – all the more because it was virtually his sole distraction in the depths of boredom.

Yet there were times when he realized what he lost as a result of this inner dependency. He sensed that everything he did was only a game; something to help him through this larval stage of school life. It had no connection with his true nature, which would only emerge later, at some as yet remote and undecided time in the future.

Whenever he saw how seriously his friends took all of this, he felt his sense of reason rebelling. He would have liked to make fun of them, but was afraid there might be more to these fantasies of theirs than he was capable of understanding. In a sense he was torn between two worlds: the respectable bourgeois world, the one he was used to at home, in which everything was ordered rationally and according to clear rules; and another one, which was bizarre, inhabited by darkness, mystery, blood and undreamt-of happenings. They seemed to be mutually exclusive. The sardonic smile that he would have liked to wear permanently somewhat contradicted a shiver that ran down his spine. Hence the thoughts that were flitting through his mind…

He longed to feel something certain in himself; definite needs that could help distinguish between good and bad, useful and not useful; to know how to make a choice, even if it was the wrong one – anything was better than this state of over-impressionability in which he simply absorbed everything…

As he walked into the little room this inner dichotomy seized hold of him again, as it always did when he came here.

Meanwhile Reiting had begun telling them what they had come to hear: Basini owed him money, and kept putting off paying him back; each time he had given his word of honour. "It doesn't bother me that much," said Reiting. "The longer it goes on, the more control I have over him. But breaking your word three or four times is no trifling matter, is it? In the end I needed the money myself. I mentioned this, and he gave me his solemn word – which he didn't keep that time either, of course. So I threatened to report him. He begged for two more days, because he was expecting a package from his guardian. In the meantime I made enquiries into his circumstances; I wanted to know if he had any other debts – after all, you should always do your homework, shouldn't you?

"I wasn't exactly overjoyed at what I discovered. He already owed Dschjusch and one or two others. He had paid back some of it, using the money I lent him, of course. The others had him over a barrel. That annoyed me. Did he take me for a soft touch? I wasn't impressed. But then I said to myself: 'Wait and see. You're bound to find an opportunity to teach him the error of his ways.' In fact one day he happened to mention the amount that he was expecting to arrive in the post, just to reassure me, since it was more than what he owed me. So I asked around and realized that it wouldn't be enough to cover all his debts by a long way. 'Aha,' I thought, 'he'll be trying it on with me again.'

"And sure enough he came to speak to me in private, and asked me to be patient a little longer, because the others were hounding him. This time I was quite frosty: 'Go and beg the others then,' I told him. 'I'm not in the habit of taking second place.'

"'But I know you better than them,' he replied, in a last-ditch attempt. 'I trust you more.'

"'This is my last word,' I said. 'Either you bring me the money tomorrow or I'll impose conditions.'

"'What conditions?' he asked. You should have heard him! It was as if he was ready to sell his soul!

"'What are my conditions? Aha! You must promise to be my loyal lieutenant in all my ventures.'

"'Really, is that all? Of course I'll do it – I'd be delighted to be on your side.'

"'Oh no, not just if it pleases *you*; you'll have to do whatever I tell you – blind obedience!'

"Then he gave me an odd look, part grin, part embarrassment. He wasn't sure what he was letting himself in for, or how serious I was. I expect he would have promised to do anything, but he must have been afraid that I would put him to the test straight away. In the end he just went red and said: 'I'll bring you the money.' It amused me actually; he was someone I'd never really noticed before, among the fifty or so others. You could say that he didn't add up to much. And then all of a sudden he was so close that I could see every detail. Obviously I was in no doubt that he was prepared to sell himself; and without too much fuss either, as long as no one else found out. It was quite a revelation I can tell you, there's nothing better than seeing someone reveal themselves like that: their true behaviour, which has always gone unnoticed, is suddenly laid out before you like the little tunnels made by woodworm when a piece of timber splits in two...

"The next day he brought me the money as promised. In fact better than that, he invited me for a drink at the restaurant in town. He ordered wine, cakes, cigarettes, and asked me to accept them as a sign of 'gratitude' for my forbearance. What I didn't like was that he was acting so innocently – as if there had never been a cross word between us. I pointed this out; but he just became nicer and nicer. It was as if he were trying to escape from my grasp, to put himself on an equal footing with me. He behaved as if everything were forgotten, and never stopped assuring me that he would always be my friend; but there was something in his eyes that gripped me, as if he were afraid that this elaborate pretence of camaraderie would soon evaporate. In the end he just disgusted me. And I thought: 'Does he really think I'm going to allow myself to be treated like this?' So I tried to think of a way of teaching him a lesson. Something that would cut him to the quick. Then suddenly I remembered that that same morning, Beineberg had told me that he had had some money stolen. The thought just came to me for no apparent reason, but it wouldn't go away. My throat had gone quite dry. 'It couldn't have come at a better time,' I thought, and so I asked him casually how much money he had left. When he told me I did a quick calculation, and the figures added up. 'So in spite of everything, who's still stupid enough to lend you more money?' I laughed. And he replied: 'Hofmeier.'

"I was so delighted that I think I must have been trembling. Only two hours before, Hofmeier had asked me to lend him some money. So the thought that had passed through my mind a few minutes earlier had suddenly become reality. It was like looking at a house and saying to oneself, jokingly: 'This house is about to catch fire,' and the next second flames are shooting into the sky...

"Very quickly I went over the various possibilities again in my mind; I admit that at that point I wasn't absolutely certain, but what my instinct told me was enough. I leant forward and said to him in the most courteous way possible, as if I were gently driving a thin, pointed stake into his brain: 'Look here, Basini my dear fellow, why are you lying to me?' As I said it his eyes seemed to be afloat in a sea of anxiety, but I pressed on: 'You might be able to fool some people, but I'm not one of them. You know very well that Beineberg...' His face didn't change colour at all, it was as if he were waiting for a misunderstanding to be cleared up. 'To cut a long story short,' I went on, 'the money you used to pay me back was money that you stole from Beineberg's locker last night!'

"Then I sat back to observe his reaction. He went as red as a beetroot; in his struggle to find a reply he began foaming at the mouth; finally he managed to get the words out. It was a stream of accusations directed at me: how dare I make such suggestions? Did I have the slightest evidence to justify such disgraceful assertions? I was just trying to pick a quarrel with him because he was weaker than me; I was only angry because paying back the money he owed me meant I no longer had a hold over him; but he was going to tell the whole class... the prefects... the headmaster; as God was his witness he was innocent, and so on and so forth *ad infinitum*. And I began to get genuinely worried that

I had accused him wrongly and upset him for no reason, because his face had turned such a bright shade of red… he looked like a defenceless little animal being tormented. But I couldn't bear the thought of giving up so easily. So as I listened to what he had to say I kept smiling my mocking smile – although it was actually just one of embarrassment. Occasionally I nodded and said quietly: 'Yes, I'm aware of that.'

"After a while he calmed down. I carried on smiling. I had the feeling that my smile alone was enough to make him a thief, even if he wasn't. And I thought: 'There'll be time to arrange that later.'

"A few more minutes went by, during which he gave me the odd furtive glance, and then all of a sudden he went pale. His air of innocent charm seemed to vanish along with the colour in his cheeks. He was now a greenish shade, whey-faced and puffy. I'd only ever seen something like that once before – when I happened to walk past as a murderer was arrested in the street. He had been mingling with the crowd too, without anyone paying the slightest attention to him. But when the constable put his hand on his shoulder he immediately became a completely different person. His features were transformed, his eyes bulged with fright and searched desperately for a way out – it was the face of a real gallows bird.

"That was what the change in Basini's expression reminded me of. So now I knew; all I had to do was wait…

"I didn't have to wait for long. Without another word from me, Basini – who had been pushed to the brink by my silence – burst into tears, and begged me to have mercy. He had only taken the money out of dire necessity; if I hadn't found out he would have put the money back before anyone was any the wiser. I ought not to call it stealing – he had simply borrowed it without anyone knowing… but he couldn't carry on, because he was crying too much…

"Then he started pleading with me again. He would be my obedient servant, do whatever I wanted, as long as I didn't tell anyone. For this he was willing to be my slave, and the combination of guile and greedy, grasping fear that was writhing around in his eyes was repulsive to behold. So I promised to give some thought to what was going to happen to him, but in the first instance it was a matter for Beineberg. So what do you both think we should do with him?"

Törless had listened to Reiting's account with his eyes closed, not saying a word. Every now and then he shuddered to the tips of his toes, while wild, unruly thoughts jostled and exploded in his head like bubbles in a pan of boiling water. It is said that this is what happens the first time you see a woman who is destined to drag you into a destructive passion; that there is a moment between two people when the soul withdraws into itself, gathers its strength, holds its breath, a moment of outer silence that conceals a state of inner tension. There is no way of knowing what really happens at such times. It could be described as a shadow cast by passion. A living, all-encompassing shadow; an easing of the tension that has gone before, and at the same time a new and sudden constraint which contains everything that is yet to come; a period of incubation so concentrated that it seems like the prick of a needle... Yet which is also a void, a vague, uncertain sensation, a feeling of weakness, anxiety...

This is what Törless was experiencing. When he stopped to think about it, Reiting's account of what had happened between him and Basini seemed of no consequence. A misdemeanour brought about by spinelessness and a lack of judgement on Basini's part, which would inevitably be followed by some vicious whim of Reiting's. But at the same time he had an alarming premonition that events had taken a distinctly personal turn, that they would affect him directly, and that there was something dangerous about this incident, which was pointing at him like the tip of a rapier.

He couldn't stop himself from imagining Basini with Božena, and glanced round the room. The walls seemed to be bearing down on him, threatening him, clutching at him with bloody hands; the revolver was swinging back and forth on its hook...

For the first time it was as if a stone had fallen into the lonely, ambivalent well of his dreams; it was just there: there was nothing he could do about it. It was reality. Yesterday Basini had been exactly the same as him, and then a trapdoor had opened and Basini had fallen down it. Exactly like in Reiting's description: there was a sudden change and the man had changed completely...

Again this seemed to create a connection with Božena. His thoughts had blasphemed. The rank, sickly smell that rose from them had confused and unsettled him. And this humiliation, this self-abnegation, this submergence beneath the pale, stifling, poisonous leaves of ignominy that floated through his dreams like a distant, ethereal reflection in a mirror – Basini had actually experienced it.

So was it really something to be reckoned with, to guard against, in case it suddenly leapt out of the silent mirror of your thoughts?...

If this were true, then everything else was possible too. Reiting and Beineberg were possible. This room was possible... And it was also possible that, in the bright, sunlit everyday world, the only one he had known up till now, there was a gateway to another world, a world that was stifling, unchained, impassioned, naked and destructive. That between those people whose well-regulated lives revolve around their work and family – as if within a solid, transparent wall of iron and glass – and the others – the fallen and bleeding who lead sordid, dissipated existences and wander through labyrinths filled with shrieking voices – there isn't simply a crossing point: their borders are actually drawing closer together, constantly and secretly, until they finally meet...

And so the only question was this: how is it possible? What really happens at moments like that? Which of them flies high into the sky, screaming, and which one dies away?...

These were the questions that this incident caused Törless to ask himself. They surged up in his mind, confused and indistinct, their lips firmly sealed, veiled by a vague, uncertain feeling that was perhaps weakness, perhaps fear...

And yet many of these words, which seemed to echo in incoherent isolation in the distance, filled him with fearful anticipation.

It was at this moment that Reiting asked his question.

Immediately Törless began to speak. He was obeying a sudden impulse, a form of dismay. He felt as if something decisive were about to happen, and was terrified at the thought that it was almost upon him; he wanted to escape, play for time... Yet even as he spoke he was aware that what he was saying was metaphorical, that his words had no inner coherence and didn't express what he really believed.

"Basini is a thief," he said. He enjoyed the firm, decisive sound of the word so much that he repeated it: "A thief. And people like that are punished everywhere in the world. He should be reported and thrown out! Let him go somewhere else and mend his ways, he doesn't belong here any more!"

Reiting reacted with surprised hostility: "No," he said. "Why should we go to extremes straight away?"

"Why? Don't you think it would be the right thing to do?"

"Absolutely not. You talk as if fire and brimstone will descend on us if we allow Basini to stay here a minute longer. What he did wasn't so terrible."

"How can you say that? You're perfectly happy to go on living, eating and sleeping under the same roof as someone who steals, who offered to be your slave! I don't understand that at all. If we're educated together, it's because we belong to the same part of society. Doesn't it bother you that one day you might find yourself in the same regiment as him, or in the same government department, moving in the same circles? That he might even pay court to your sister?..."

"Come off it, aren't you getting rather carried away?" laughed Reiting. "You're behaving as if we're part of a lifelong fraternity! Do you think we've all been stamped with a special seal that says: 'Former pupil of W. Endowed with special privileges and duties'? We'll all go our separate ways eventually; each of us will get his due reward in life, because there's no such thing as one single society. What I mean is that we shouldn't agonize about the future. As for the present, I'm not suggesting that we continue to be friends with Basini. There will always be ways of maintaining a distance between him and us. Basini is under our control, we can do what we like with him; you can spit in his face night and morning as far as I'm concerned, if that's what pleases you: as long as he puts up with it, what common ground is there between us? And if he rebels, we can still show him who's in charge... Forget the idea that there's a bond between ourselves and Basini, apart from the amusement his despicable character will provide!"

Although Törless himself was far from convinced by his own argument, he became increasingly agitated: "Listen, Reiting, why are you so keen to take Basini's side?"

"Is that what I'm doing? I'm not so sure. I don't have any reason to do so: in fact the whole business leaves me indifferent. But what does annoy me is that you're exaggerating. What's got into you? Some sort of idealism I expect. Saintly devotion to the Old School or justice. You can't imagine how soppy and oh-so commendable it sounds. Or maybe" – and Reiting narrowed his eyes and gave Törless a suspicious look – "there's some other reason why Basini has to be thrown out, but you don't want to put your cards on the table? Some old score you want to settle? So tell us! If it's worth the effort this might be the ideal opportunity to make use of it."

Törless turned to Beineberg. But the latter was just smirking. While the other two were talking he had been sitting with his legs crossed oriental fashion, dragging on a long chibouk; with his protruding ears, in the ambivalent light he resembled a monstrous idol. "As far as I'm concerned you can do what you like," he said. "I'm not worried about money or justice. In India they would drive a sharpened bamboo cane into his belly; at least that would have the virtue of being entertaining. He's stupid and cowardly, so he wouldn't be any great loss, and not once in my life have I been remotely concerned about what happens to people of his sort. In themselves they're nothing, and as for what becomes of their souls, we have no idea. May Allah bless your decision!"

Törless didn't reply. Now that Reiting had contradicted him and Beineberg refused to influence their decision, he had nothing more to say. He wasn't capable of further resistance: in fact he sensed that he no longer had any desire to hold back the dark, obscure events that were about to take place.

So when Reiting made a suggestion it was agreed. It was decided that for the time being Basini would be kept under observation, effectively under supervision, to give him the chance to make amends. His income and expenditure would be strictly monitored, and his dealings with other pupils subject to approval by the three of them.

This decision had all the appearances of being correct and well intentioned – "soppy and oh-so commendable" as Reiting would have said, although this time he didn't. In fact, although they didn't admit as much to each other, they all sensed that what they ought to establish now was a form of interregnum. Because of the pleasure it afforded him, Reiting would have been reluctant not to see the matter through to its conclusion, although as yet he wasn't sure what direction events might take. As for Törless, the thought that he would have to associate with Basini on a daily basis left him in something like a state of paralysis.

When he used the word "thief" earlier, it had brought him a moment of relief. As if everything that was gnawing away inside him had been thrust aside, ejected.

But the questions that immediately resurfaced couldn't be answered by this one word alone. At the same time as becoming clearer they were now even more unavoidable.

He looked first at Reiting, then at Beineberg, closed his eyes, repeated the details of their decision to himself, then opened his eyes again... He was no longer sure if it was his imagination that seemed to have placed an enormous distorting lens between him and all these things, or whether what was taking shape in front of him in such a sinister way was actually real. Were Beineberg and Reiting the only ones who were unaware of these questions? Despite the fact that they had always been at home in this world, which for the first time was beginning to seem so strange to him?

Törless was afraid of them. But only in the sense that you are afraid of a giant that you know is blind and stupid...

One thing was certain, however: he had come a long way in the last quarter of an hour. Turning back was no longer possible. Now he had committed himself against his will he began to feel curious about what was going to happen. Everything that was stirring and muttering deep inside him was still shrouded in mystery, yet he felt a growing desire to stare into this darkness and see the shapes it contained, shapes that the others never noticed. Mingling with this desire was a faint trembling, as if from now on an ashen and overcast sky would hang continuously over his life – a sky filled with enormous clouds, vast, constantly changing shapes, and always the same question over and over again: are they monsters, or just clouds?

And this question was for him alone to answer! It was secret, alien and forbidden territory to the others...

For the first time, the significance that Basini would later assume in Törless's life began to become apparent.

The next day Basini was placed under supervision.

Not without certain ceremony. They chose a morning gymnastics period out on the playing fields, which they had managed to skip.

Reiting gave a form of address – which wasn't exactly brief. He pointed out to Basini that he had brought his own character into disrepute, that he should have been reported, and that he owed it to an exceptional act of mercy on their part that for the moment he was spared the disgrace of being expelled.

He was then informed of the special conditions. Reiting took it upon himself to ensure that they were adhered to.

Throughout this little scene Basini remained very pale, but he didn't say a word, and it was impossible to tell from his expression what he was thinking or feeling.

Törless found the whole performance in turns extremely tasteless and enormously significant.

Beineberg, meanwhile, paid far more attention to Reiting than to Basini.

5

DURING THE DAYS that followed, the whole affair seemed to have been virtually forgotten. Apart from during lessons and at mealtimes, Reiting was hardly ever seen, and Beineberg was more taciturn than ever, while Törless tried constantly to put the matter out of his mind.

As for Basini, he came and went among all the others as if nothing had happened.

He was slightly taller than Törless, rather puny, with limp, languid movements and a girlish face. Although not particularly intelligent and one of the weakest at fencing and gymnastics, there was nonetheless a quite winning, flirtatious charm about him.

He only went to Božena in order to put on an act of manliness. As a late developer, he was unlikely to have experienced any genuine desire. He probably felt obliged to do it out of good form and duty, to ensure that he didn't lack an aura of amorous experience. For him the best part was when he walked out of Božena's room and left it all behind, because for him the most important thing was to acquire the souvenir.

There were also times when he would lie out of pure vanity. After the holidays he always returned to school with mementoes of his various escapades – ribbons, locks of hair, billets-doux. But when he came back with a garter in his trunk, a small, delightfully fragrant, pale-blue garter that later transpired to belong to his twelve-year-old sister, he was ridiculed for such absurd braggadocio.

His evident lack of moral fibre went hand in hand with foolish behaviour. Easily led, he never failed to be surprised at the consequences of his actions. In this he resembled a woman with kiss curls arranged over her forehead who puts a small dose of poison in all of her husband's food, and is then horrified at the judge's harsh words as he pronounces the death sentence.

Törless avoided him. As a result, the profound shock that from the first moment had shaken his thoughts to their very roots gradually lost its grip. Everything around him became rational and well ordered again; as the days went by his discomfiture faded into the realms of illusion, like the last vestiges of a dream that is unable to hold out against the solid, sunlit reality of the world.

As a way of reassuring himself that the situation would be maintained, he wrote to his parents and told them what had happened. The only details he left out were his own feelings.

He now felt, as he had originally, that it would be best if Basini were to be expelled as soon as possible. To him it was inconceivable that his parents could think otherwise. He expected them to condemn Basini in the strongest, most disgusted terms, in the way one might brush away an unpleasant insect to prevent it from coming anywhere near one's child.

There was nothing of this in the reply that he received. Being reasonable, upright people they had gone to great lengths to consider all the circumstances, inasmuch as they were able to form a picture of them from the sketchy information in his hastily written letter. Thus they favoured the most lenient and measured response, all the more so because they knew their son's account was likely to be influenced by the exaggerations of indignant youth. They approved of the decision to give Basini an opportunity to reform, and were of the view that no one had the right to ruin a person's chances in life on account of a minor lapse. Especially – and they stressed this point particularly – when dealing with people who were not fully grown, whose characters were still developing and thus malleable. Of course, Basini had to be dealt with severely, but always with kindness, so as to encourage him to mend his ways.

They reinforced their remarks with a series of examples that were very familiar to him. He still had vivid memories of his first few years at the school, when the masters were fond of draconian measures, imposing strict limits on pocket money, and many of the younger boys, gluttonous creatures that they were, were unable to resist scrounging a piece of ham sandwich or something similar from their more fortunate classmates.

He hadn't always been able to avoid the temptation himself, although he concealed his shame by grumbling about the malicious, evil-minded masters. It wasn't just the process of growing up, but also the well-intentioned urgings of his parents, that had taught him to put pride before such weakness.

But this no longer had the desired effect.

He had to admit that in many respects his parents were right, although he knew it was almost impossible for them to judge from a distance. But their letter seemed to lack something even more important.

This missing element was the awareness that something irreparable had happened, something that ought never to happen among people of a certain milieu. They spoke as if it were perfectly normal, that it simply had to be handled with tact and sensitivity and without making a fuss. A blemish, yes, but only a minor one, and as inevitable as a call of nature. There was no more evidence of concern or personal perceptions in their letter than there was in Beineberg or Reiting.

Törless could have left it at that. But he tore the letter into little pieces and burned it. It was the first time in his life that he had shown such a lack of filial respect.

Their letter had quite the opposite effect to what had been intended. In contrast with the simple, commonsensical opinions that he had been offered, it was the more ambiguous and dubious aspects of Basini's misconduct which came flooding into his mind. Shaking his head, he told himself that he would have to give it more thought, although he couldn't think of any reason why.

The strangest thing of all was when his thoughts were followed by dreams. Basini would appear to him exactly as he did every day, clear and comprehensible, the same as his parents and friends might have seen him. But the next moment he would vanish, only to keep reappearing as a tiny little figure that glowed faintly in the background, far far away...

6

T HEN LATE ONE NIGHT, when everyone was asleep, he
suddenly felt someone shaking him.

Beineberg was sitting beside his bed. It was so unusual that
he immediately guessed it must be something serious.

"Get up. And don't make a noise: we don't want anyone to
notice. We've got to go upstairs, there's something I have to
tell you."

Törless threw on some clothes, found a coat and jammed his
feet into his slippers…

When they got to the attic, Beineberg took particular care to
replace all the obstacles behind them, and then made some tea.

Still half-asleep, Törless contentedly let the warm, fragrant,
golden-ochre fluid course its way through his body. Curled up
in a corner, he was looking forward to being astonished.

Eventually Beineberg said: "Reiting is betraying us."

Törless wasn't remotely surprised; it was obvious that the
situation was going to take a turn of this kind; it was almost as
if he had been waiting for it to happen. Instinctively he burst
out: "Just as I thought!"

"Oh, you thought, did you? But of course you didn't actually
see anything? That's you all over."

"I admit I didn't notice anything in particular; but then it
wasn't exactly at the front of my mind."

"Meanwhile I was keeping my eyes open: I never trusted Reiting
from day one. You know Basini gave me my money back, of
course. And where do you think it came from? Him? No."

"And you think Reiting had something to do with it?"

"Definitely."

At first Törless assumed that Reiting was involved in the same
sort of thing as Basini.

"So you think Reiting was… doing the same as Basini?…"

"Don't be ridiculous! Reiting gave Basini just enough money out of his own pocket so he could pay his debts to me."

"But I don't see what reason he would have for doing that."

"Neither did I for a while. But you must have noticed, as I did, how from the very beginning Reiting was so keen to stand up for Basini. And you were absolutely right: the proper thing would have been for him to be thrown out immediately. But I made a point of not supporting you at the time, because I was thinking to myself: 'I want to see what his little game is.' To be honest I wasn't sure if Reiting had any precise intentions at that point, or if he simply wanted to wait till he could be totally sure about Basini. But I know now exactly how things stand."

"And?"

"Don't be in such a hurry, I'll come to that in a minute. Do you remember that business at the school four years ago?"

"What business?"

"You know, that one."

"Only vaguely. All I remember is there was a big scandal because of some disgusting behaviour or other, and that quite a few people were expelled."

"That's it. During one holiday I found out more details from someone who used to be in that class. There was a pretty boy who a lot of them were in love with. You know what I mean; it happens every year. Only this time they went a bit too far."

"In what way?"

"In what way? Don't pretend you don't know what I'm talking about! And that's what Reiting is doing with Basini!"

Törless knew exactly what Beineberg meant. He thought he was going to choke, as if he had swallowed a mouthful of sand.

"I'd never have believed it of Reiting." He wasn't sure what else to say. Beineberg shrugged.

"He thinks he can deceive us."

"Is he in love with him?"

"Not in the least. He's no fool. It just amuses him, or gives him a thrill, nothing more than that."

"What about Basini?"

"Him?... Haven't you noticed how cheeky he's been getting? He hardly takes any notice of a word I say. It's always Reiting this and Reiting that – anyone would think he was his patron saint. He probably came to the conclusion that it's better to put up with everything from one person than a little bit from each of us. And Reiting will have promised to protect him as long as he lets him do whatever he likes. But they're making a mistake, because I'm going to settle Basini's hash once and for all!"

"How did you find out?"

"I followed them."

"Where?"

"To the attic next door. Reiting had my key for the other entrance. I came up here, carefully opened up the hole and crept through to where they were."

An opening had been made in the thin partition wall that separated the little room from the main attic, just wide enough for someone to squeeze through. It acted as an emergency exit in case they were taken by surprise, and was usually filled in with bricks.

There was a long pause during which all that could be heard was them drawing on their glowing cigarettes.

Törless was unable to think, but he could see... all of a sudden behind his closed eyelids he saw a wild, swirling scene... people: people lit up by a dazzling light, pools of brightness, pools of deep, almost etched-out, constantly moving shadow; faces... a face, a smile... staring eyes... trembling flesh. He saw people as he had never seen or experienced them before, and yet he saw without seeing, without imagining or summoning up their images, as if he were seeing them with the eyes of his

65

soul; they were so clear that he was pierced by their vividness as if by a thousand arrows, but as soon as he tried to find the words that would give him mastery over them they stopped, as if they had come to a threshold that they were unable to cross, and shrunk back.

He had to know more. His voice was shaking as he asked. "And… you saw?"

"Yes."

"And… Basini… what was he like?"

Beineberg didn't reply, and soon the only sound was the same faint sputtering of their cigarettes. There was another long pause, and then he began to speak again.

"I've turned the matter over in my mind, looked at it from every angle, and you know I have my own particular ideas about this. As for Basini, in my opinion he's not worth losing any sleep over. We could report him, beat him senseless or torture him half to death just for the fun of it; it doesn't really matter. Because I find it impossible to imagine where an individual like him fits in with the whole incredible mechanism of the universe. To my mind he must have been created by accident, outside the usual order of things. What I mean to say is that he must have some purpose or other, but only something vague and undecided, like a worm or a stone that you come across on the road, and you don't know whether to step over it or crush it underfoot. It's not worth mentioning. When the World Soul wants one of its individual parts to be preserved then it makes this known, clearly and unambiguously. It says no, then creates an obstacle, causes us to step over the worm and makes the stone so hard that we are unable to shatter it without using tools. But before we can go and fetch them it produces another obstacle, made up of a host of small but unshakeable doubts, and even if we manage to overcome them it's only because, right from the beginning, the obstruction had meant something completely different.

"In the case of humanity, it places this hard quality within our consciousness of being human, our innate sense of responsibility that comes from knowing that we are part of the World Soul. If a person loses this consciousness, then it is himself that he has lost. But when a human being loses himself and capitulates, he also loses those unique and special qualities for which Nature made him human. And we can never be more certain of this than when we are confronted with something that has no purpose, an empty shape that the World Soul abandoned a long time ago."

Törless had no wish to contradict him. In fact he had hardly been paying attention. Not once had he had cause to turn to metaphysical musings of this kind; nor had he ever wondered why a sensible individual like Beineberg could dream up such things. None of these questions had ever played a part in his life.

So he didn't bother to try to work out if Beineberg's arguments made sense; he was only half listening.

He couldn't understand how anyone could go back over ancient history like this. Inwardly he was all aquiver, and found the circumspect way in which Beineberg expressed thoughts that he had dug up God knows where to be utterly absurd, uncalled for and infuriating. Yet Beineberg carried on, unperturbed: "With Reiting it's another matter, of course. By doing what he's done he's played into my hands too, although naturally I'm far from indifferent to his fate, as I am to Basini's. You know that his mother doesn't have a great fortune; if he were expelled then all his plans would come to nothing. If he stays he might be able to make something of himself, but otherwise the opportunities will be few and far between. Reiting has never really liked me… you realize that, don't you?… In fact he's always hated me… in the past he's done his utmost to harm me in whatever way he can… even today I think he'd be glad to get rid of me. So don't you see what an advantage it is for me to possess this secret?…"

Törless was scared. Yet in a most peculiar way, as if what happened to Reiting affected him personally. He gave Beineberg a frightened glance. The other boy's eyes were just slits, he looked like an enormous, sinister spider sitting calmly on its web, ready to pounce. His last remarks echoed with ice-cold clarity in Törless's ears like a decree.

He hadn't been following what his friend was saying, and had simply thought: "Beineberg is just going on about his ideas again, which have nothing to do with the facts"… so he had no idea how things had reached this point.

The strands of the web, which as far as he could remember had been part of some distant abstract realm, must have drawn themselves together with astonishing speed. Because all at once it was concrete, real, alive, and a head was wriggling around inside it… its throat choked off.

He didn't have a high opinion of Reiting, but remembered the delightfully brazen, blasé manner in which he went about his many intrigues, while in comparison Beineberg disgusted him, the way he calmly and smirkingly spun this loathsome, grey, many-stranded web of thoughts around his opponent.

Without thinking, Törless burst out: "You have no right to use that against him." The secret aversion that he had always felt for Beineberg probably played a part in his reaction.

After a moment's reflection, Beineberg replied: "Yes, what would be the point? It would be a shame for him, actually. One way or another I've got nothing to fear from him now, and he doesn't deserve to come to grief over some minor act of stupidity." This dealt with one part of the problem. But then Beineberg stopped, and returned to what they ought to do with Basini.

"Do you still think we should report him?" he asked. Törless didn't reply. He just wanted to listen to Beineberg talking, the words ringing out in his head like footsteps on hollow ground; he wanted to enjoy the situation to the full.

Beineberg pursued his train of thought: "For the time being I think we should keep him here and punish him ourselves. Because he must be punished – if only for his impudence. The school would be content to expel him and write a long letter to his uncle – you know how such things generally read: 'Excellency, your nephew has had a slight lapse... went astray... we are sending him back... in the hope that you will be successful in... mend his ways... not a good influence on the other pupils at the moment... etc.' Does a case like this have the slightest interest or value for them?"

"And what value does it have for us?"

"What value? For you possibly none, since you're going to be a court counsellor or write verse; things like that aren't of any use to you; perhaps they even frighten you. But I have other plans in life!"

This time Törless pricked up his ears.

"Basini has value for me – a great one even. Of course you would simply let him go, and comfort yourself with the thought that he was a bad lot." Törless had to stop himself from smiling. "As far as you're concerned that's the end of the matter, because you have neither the talent nor the interest to learn lessons from a case like this. But me, I am interested. When you're intending to take the direction in life that I am, you have to have a quite different view of people. Which is why I intend to keep Basini for myself, to learn from him."

"But how are you going to punish him?"

Beineberg didn't reply immediately, as if he were weighing up the likely impact of what he was about to say. Then, cautiously and a little hesitantly, he said: "If you think I'm eager to punish him then you're mistaken. Of course, you could regard what I'm proposing as a form of punishment... but, to cut a long story short, I have something else in mind, I want to... how shall we say... torment him..."

Törless was careful not to say anything. Although it wasn't yet clear to him, he sensed that events were unfolding as they were meant to for him, for the person deep down inside him. Unable to appreciate the effect that his remarks had had, Beineberg went on: "There's no need to be alarmed, it's not as terrible as all that. In the first place, as I've already explained, we don't have to take Basini into consideration at all. Any decision to torment or spare him depends only on the need we might feel to do one or the other of those things: on our inner motives. Do you follow? As for what you were saying the other day about morality, society and so forth, none of that matters of course; I hope you never actually believed it yourself. So presumably such things are a matter of indifference to you. All the same, there's still time to pull out if you're not prepared to take the risk.

"For me there's no going back or sidestepping, the path leads straight ahead. Which is how it has to be. Reiting isn't going to give up either: it's important for him to have someone under his control, to exercise his will over, to treat like some sort of instrument. He wants to rule, and if the opportunity arose he would treat *you* exactly as he does Basini. For me it's much more than that: almost a commitment that I've made to myself. How can I explain the difference between us? You know how much Reiting worships Napoleon; whereas for me, the person I admire the most is more likely to be a philosopher or an Indian holy man. Reiting would sacrifice Basini purely out of curiosity. He would dissect his soul just to discover what the process involves. And as I said, it makes not the slightest difference to him whether he uses you, me or Basini. I, on the other hand, have similar feelings to yours: that when all is said and done Basini is still a human being. Committing such acts of cruelty would offend my own sensibilities as well. But that's exactly what this is about! Sacrifice! Don't you see that I'm torn in two directions: one, which is ill defined, binds me, contrary to my strongest convictions, to a compassionate passivity, while the other, which appeals to my soul, to the most profound inner knowledge, ties me to the Cosmos. As I said earlier, people like Basini are of no significance – they are empty shapes created by chance. The only true people are those who enter deeply into themselves, cosmic beings who are capable of descending far enough to discover their connection with the vast inner workings of the universe. They perform miracles with their eyes closed, because they know how to make use of every power that the world possesses, powers that exist within as well as around them. But up till now, those who have been travelling in the second direction have always had to break away from the first. I've read about the horrific acts of penitence performed by enlightened monks, and I'm sure the practices of Hindu ascetics aren't unknown to you. All these appalling acts of cruelty have but one purpose: to mortify the miserable worldly desires which – whether vanity or hunger, joy or compassion – only serve to smother the flames that each of us has the capacity to kindle within ourselves.

"Reiting is only familiar with the external world, while I am taking the second path. Everyone else believes he has a head start on me at the moment, because my road is slower and more uncertain. Yet with one bound I could leave him far behind, like a worm. As you know, people claim that the world is made up of unshakeable physical laws. But that's completely wrong, the stuff of textbooks! No doubt the outside world is unsentimental in its outlook, and to a degree its so-called laws won't brook any interference, but there have been individuals who have managed to do so. This is contained in sacred texts that have been much studied, but which most people have no knowledge of. From reading these I know that there were once men who were able to move rocks, the sky and the seas simply through an act of will, and whose prayers were too strong for any power on earth to withstand. Yet that too is only an external triumph of the spirit. Because those who have succeeded in seeing their soul *in its entirety* are detached from their bodily existence, which is only incidental; it says in the sacred books that such people enter a higher spiritual realm."

Beineberg spoke with complete conviction, while controlling his emotions. Törless had kept his eyes closed almost the whole time; he could feel the other boy's breath flowing over him, and inhaled it like an oppressive drug. In the meantime, Beineberg arrived at his conclusion:

"So you can see what this means for me. Whatever is trying to persuade me to leave Basini in peace is primitive and external in origin. Obey it if you wish. But for me it's a prejudice from which I must free myself, along with everything else that causes me to stray from the Inner Path.

"The very fact that I find it difficult to torment Basini – what I mean to say is humiliate him, grind him into the dirt, thrust him away from me – is good. It demands a sacrifice. It will have a purifying effect. It's due to him that I learn every day that merely being human is of no significance – that it's nothing more than an apelike, superficial appearance."

Törless didn't understand everything that he had heard. As before, he just had the impression that an invisible noose had suddenly tightened into a very real and lethal knot. Beineberg's last remark was still echoing inside his head, and he repeated it to himself: "An apelike, superficial appearance." This seemed to describe his relationship with Basini. Didn't the strange fascination that the latter exerted over him consist of visions such as these? Of the fact that he simply wasn't able to put himself in Basini's position, which was why he experienced him in the form of hazy images? When he had tried to picture Basini earlier, behind his face hadn't there been another one, blurred and indistinct? A face that bore a striking resemblance to the other one, and yet which was somehow unidentifiable.

So instead of reflecting on Beineberg's bizarre intentions, and overcome by all these new and unusual impressions, Törless devoted his efforts to examining his inner self more closely. He remembered the afternoon before he had found out about Basini's theft. Even then the visions were already there. There was always something that his thoughts were not quite able to identify; something simple and yet unfamiliar. He had seen images that weren't really images. The little peasant houses by the roadside, even himself and Beineberg in the patisserie.

There were similarities and irreconcilable differences at one and the same time. And this game, this secret, totally personal perspective had excited him.

And now a person was attracting all this towards himself. It all took human form, became real and alive, and all its strangeness was transferred onto that person. In doing so it left the imaginary world and entered that of the living, became a threat.

But this state of agitation wearied him, and he lost the train of his thoughts. All that remained was the idea that he mustn't let go of this person Basini, that he was sure to play an important, but as yet undecided part in his life.

When he remembered what Beineberg had said, he shook his head in amazement. So was he... as well?...

He can't possibly be looking for the same thing as I am, and yet he's found exactly the right words to describe it...

Törless was not so much thinking as dreaming. He was no longer able to distinguish between his own psychological problems and Beineberg's delusions. All he was left with was the feeling that the gigantic noose was getting tighter and tighter.

The conversation went no further. They put out the lamp and crept back to the dormitory.

7

T HE NEXT FEW DAYS brought no decision. They had too much work to do, Reiting went out of his way to avoid being alone with either of them, and even Beineberg appeared to rule out any further discussion.

During this time, recent events etched themselves even deeper into Törless's soul, like a stream diverted from its natural course, channelling his thoughts in a direction from which there was no turning back.

Any idea of having Basini expelled was abandoned once and for all. For the first time Törless felt totally concentrated on himself, and was incapable of thinking about anything else. Božena too had become a matter of indifference to him; what he had once felt for her was now no more than a fanciful memory, replaced by utter seriousness.

Admittedly this seriousness didn't seem to be any less fanciful.

Deep in thought, he went for a walk in the grounds. It was the middle of the day, and a late-autumn sun cast faint memories of summer over the lawns and pathways. In his restless mood he felt no desire to go very far, so he just walked round the corner of the building and threw himself down on the faded, rustling grass at the foot of the almost windowless lateral wall. The sky stretched out above him, that washed-out, sorrowful shade of blue that autumn makes its own, with small, white, crumpled clouds scurrying across it.

He lay on his back, blinking, his vague, dreamy gaze drifting between the tops of two almost leafless trees nearby.

His thoughts turned to Beineberg; what a peculiar person he was! His words belonged in some crumbling Hindu temple, along with sinister idols and sorcerer snakes in the depths of dark caves; but not in broad daylight in a school in modern-day

Europe! And yet, having found their way along a series of end-less, tortuously winding paths, his words seemed to have come to a sudden and concrete conclusion...

Then suddenly, as if for the first time, he noticed how high the sky was.

It was almost frightening. Between the clouds immediately above him there glowed a small, blue, unimaginably deep hole.

He was sure it would be possible to reach it using a long, long ladder. But the farther he travelled into the heights, the higher his eyes carried him, the more the bright-blue depths retreated. And yet one must have been able to climb up there at least once and fix one's gaze on it. And this desire began to torment him.

It was as if his vision, stretched to its very limits, was shoot-ing dart-like glances through the clouds, and yet however far they reached they always fell short.

He began to reflect on this, while trying to remain as calm and rational as possible. "It really does seem to go on for ever," he thought. "It stretches on and on without stopping, all the way to infinity." As he said this he kept his gaze fixed on the sky, as if he were testing the power of a magic charm. But to no avail: the words meant nothing, or rather they meant something different, as if they were talking about the same object from an unfamiliar and unimportant angle.

"Infinity!" He remembered the word from maths lessons. He had never imagined it as anything special. It was always coming up; ever since it was invented people had been able to use it in calculations the same as any other tangible object. It was worth whatever it was worth in the relevant calculation; he had never attempted to discover any more about it than that.

And then it struck him that there was something alarming associated with this word. It gave the impression of being a tame concept that he could use in everyday sleights of hand, but which had now been unleashed. Something wild, irrational and destructive that seemed to have been lulled to sleep by the machinations of an inventor had suddenly woken and reassumed its former terrifying aspect. It was up there in the sky, very much alive, threatening and mocking him.

In the end he had to close his eyes because he couldn't bear to look at it.

Shortly afterwards, when he was woken by a gust of wind rustling through the dry grass, he could hardly feel his body, and a pleasant coolness wafted up from around his feet, filling him with a soft, mellow lethargy. The fear that he had felt was joined by a sensation of gentle weariness. He could still feel the sky gazing down at him in all its silence and vastness, but now remembered that it had often had this effect on him in the past and, as if drifting between waking and dreaming, he went back over his memories, sensing that he was caught in their web.

The first of these was from childhood, in which trees stood around him in grave-faced silence, like people under a spell. Even at the time he must have already experienced this sensation, which would later keep coming back to him. Even the ideas he had when he was with Božena contained an element of this, something particular and prescient, and more significant than it at first seemed. The moment of utter silence in the garden outside the patisserie window had been the same, before the dark veil of sensuality descended. And often, for a split second, Beineberg and Reiting would also be transformed into something strange, unreal – and Basini? The mental picture of what had happened with him had left Törless deeply divided; one minute it was perfectly rational and mundane, the next it was infiltrated by the image-laden silence that all these impressions shared, and which gradually permeated his consciousness until it was demanding to be treated as something real and alive; exactly as he had imagined the concept of infinity.

He sensed that it was closing in on him from all sides. It had probably been there all the time, like a dark, distant, menacing power, but he had instinctively shied away and only given it the odd fearful glance. Yet a chance event had made him pay attention to it and, as if at a signal, it now burst in on him from every direction, dragging in its wake a terrible confusion that kept growing and growing.

He was seized by a madness to experience things, events and people as something ambiguous; something that the power of an inventor had linked to an innocent explanatory term yet which threatened to become something unfamiliar that might burst forth at any second.

Of course, he was aware that there was a simple explanation for everything, but to his horrified amazement it seemed as if it were only an outer layer that had been torn away without exposing what lay within, which, with a gaze that had become almost unnatural, he could see glimmering in the depths.

So he just lay there, wrapped up in memories, out of which strange ideas grew like unfamiliar flowers. All those moments that no one can ever forget, situations that have lost the coherence that allows our life to be a mirror image of our reason, as if the two things run in parallel and at the same speed, now became completely entangled.

The memory of the terrifying, motionless silence, the mournful colours of certain evenings alternated seamlessly with the hot, feverish agitation of a noonday in summer that had passed glowingly over his soul like a swarm of scurrying, iridescent lizards.

Suddenly he remembered the way the young prince had once smiled at him, a certain look, a gesture he had made around the time that their friendship was coming to an end, and which with a single – gentle – stroke cut through the feelings of affinity that

Törless had woven around him, after which he entered a new, unfamiliar world which – as if concentrated into an intense, single moment of existence – suddenly opened up in front of him. Then came more memories of the forest, along with those of the open countryside. And then the still, silent image of a darkened room at home that had later reminded him of the friend he had lost. The words of a poem echoed in his mind...

And there are many other things in which this same sense of the immeasurable also prevails, between experience and understanding. Yet it is always the case that whatever we experience fleetingly and unthinkingly as universal becomes incomprehensible and bewildering the moment we try to shackle it with the chain of our thoughts and take possession of it. And what appears vast and unfathomable as long as our words reach out to grasp it from a distance becomes simple and loses its ability to unsettle us once it enters the domain of everyday life.

And all these memories suddenly shared the same mystery. They were standing right in front of him, as if they belonged together, so close that he could reach out and touch them.

Whenever they had come to him in the past they had been accompanied by an obscure feeling to which he had paid little attention.

That feeling was what he was now endeavouring to recapture. He remembered a day when he and his father were looking at a landscape, and he had suddenly exclaimed: "Oh, it's so beautiful!" and was embarrassed when this had pleased his father. Because he might as well have said, "It's terribly sad." It was this failure of words which tormented him, a vague awareness that they were only incidental, a pale imitation of emotions.

And now he remembered the images, the words and, most vividly of all, the feeling that he was lying, without knowing why. Again his gaze travelled back through his memories; and again it came back without any solutions. The smile of delight that still hovered distractedly over his lips at this abundance of ideas began to take on a barely perceptible air of suffering.

He felt a constant need to find a bridge, a connection, some form of comparison between himself and whatever was standing silently in the way of his mind.

Yet each time he had a comforting thought, the same incomprehensible objection was still there: "You are lying." It was as if he had to go through a continual process of long division out of which a stubborn remainder always appeared to prevent him from finishing the calculation, or he had cut his finger by feverishly struggling with a knot that resisted every attempt to untie it.

Eventually he gave up. Everything closed in around him, his memories grew until they were abnormally distorted.

He looked up at the sky again, as if by chance he might be able to snatch its secret away from it, as well as the answer to everything that was confusing him. But he soon grew weary, and a profound feeling of solitude closed in around him. The sky fell silent, and he sensed that he was completely alone beneath this mute, impassive vault, a tiny speck of life beneath an enormous transparent corpse.

But this no longer really frightened him. It was as if an old, familiar pain had now spread to the last of his healthy limbs.

The light seemed to have taken on an opaque, milky glow, and a cold, pale mist hovered in front of his eyes.

Slowly and carefully he turned his head, and looked round to see if anything had changed. His gaze travelled across the surface of the grey, windowless wall behind him. It seemed to be leaning forward and silently watching him. Every now and then something like a murmur ran down it from top to bottom, as if a sinister life form was beginning to stir.

He had often listened for this sound in the attic hideout whenever Beineberg or Reiting were parading their imaginary worlds, and had enjoyed it as if it were the incidental music for an outlandish theatrical performance.

But now even the bright sunlight seemed to have become an inaccessible hiding place, while the living silence encircled him from every direction.

He didn't have the strength to turn his gaze away. Coltsfoot was growing nearby in a damp, dark corner, its large, abundant leaves providing the perfect hiding place for worms and snails.

Törless could hear his heart beating. Then there was another faint murmuring, almost a trickling sound... These were the last signs of life in a silent world where time stood still...

8

THE NEXT DAY HE SAW Beineberg and Reiting together, and went over to them.

"I've already spoken to Reiting," said Beineberg, "and we've arranged everything. Although these things aren't of much interest to you, are they?"

Faced with this sudden turn of events, Törless felt something like rage and jealousy welling up inside him, although he wasn't sure if he should mention the previous night's conversation to Reiting. "You might at least have consulted me, seeing that I'm as involved as you are," he retorted.

"We would have done, my dear Törless," Reiting hurriedly replied, clearly keen to avoid any unnecessary difficulties, "but we couldn't find you anywhere, and we knew we could count on your agreement. So what do you think of Basini now?" (There was no hint of an apology, as if his own behaviour were a matter of course.)

"What do I think of him? He's a contemptible individual," Törless replied rather awkwardly.

"Quite. Most contemptible."

"But what you're doing isn't exactly delightful either!" And Törless gave him a slightly forced smile, because he was ashamed at not being angrier with Reiting.

"Me?" Reiting just shrugged. "What's wrong with that? One has to experience everything in life, and since he's so worthless and stupid…"

"Have you spoken to him since?" put in Beineberg.

"Yes. He came to see me yesterday evening and asked for money. He's got more debts that he can't pay."

"Did you give him any?"

"No, not yet."

"Excellent," said Beineberg. "It's the opportunity we've been waiting for. Tell him to meet you somewhere tonight."

"Where? In the room upstairs?"

"I don't think that's a good idea: it's best if he doesn't know it exists for the time being. Tell him to come to the main attic, the place where you were before."

"What time?"

"Let's say… eleven."

"Fine. Shall we carry on with our walk?"

"All right. Törless has probably got a lot to do – haven't you?"

Törless didn't have any work to do, but he sensed that the other two were keeping something to themselves and didn't wish to share it with him. He was annoyed with himself for his stand-offishness, which prevented him from forcing himself on them.

So as they walked off he just looked on in envy, wracking his brains to try to imagine what they might be secretly arranging.

At the same time he was struck by the innocent charm in Reiting's lithe yet upright way of walking – just as there was in the way he spoke. And he tried to picture him on the night in question – what had happened deep inside him. It must have been like two souls gripping each other tightly and sinking slowly down, down, into the depths of a subterranean kingdom; a brief moment when the sounds of the world far above faded away then died out completely.

Was it possible for someone to be so cheerful and light-hearted after doing something like that? It certainly didn't seem to mean much to Reiting. Törless would have very much liked to ask him! But because of his childish inhibitions he had abandoned him to the spidery Beineberg!

At a quarter to eleven that night, Törless saw Beineberg and Reiting slip out of bed, and immediately began to get dressed.

"Ssh!" whispered one of them. "Wait a minute. Someone will notice if all three of us go out at the same time."

Törless hid under the covers again.

They met in the corridor, and made their way up the stairs to the attic, taking the usual precautions.

"Where's Basini?" asked Törless.

"He's coming the other way; Reiting gave him the key."

They climbed all the way up in darkness. Only when they reached the great iron door at the top did Beineberg light his little signal lamp.

The lock refused to turn. It hadn't been opened for years, and the spare key couldn't get it to work. Eventually it gave way with a sharp clunk, and the heavy door creaked on its rusty hinges and swung open reluctantly.

From the attic came a breath of warm, stale air, like the atmosphere in a small hothouse.

Beineberg closed the door behind them.

They walked down the short flight of wooden stairs and crouched beside a massive crossbeam.

Nearby were several enormous vats of water, which were used in the event of a fire. The water obviously hadn't been changed for a long time, as it gave off a slightly sweet, sickly smell.

The whole atmosphere of the place was oppressive: the intense heat under the roof, the stifling air and the maze of huge beams, some of which disappeared into the darkness above, while others seemed to creep towards the floor in a tangle of eerie shapes.

Beineberg shaded the lamp, and for several long minutes they sat in the darkness, not moving or saying a word.

Then in the shadows at the far end the door creaked quietly and hesitantly. It was the sort of noise that makes the heart beat wildly, like the sound of approaching prey.

Next came hesitant footsteps, someone stumbling over an echoing floorboard; a dull thud like a body falling to the ground... silence... and then more uncertain footsteps... a pause... a voice calling out softly... "Reiting?"

Beineberg took the shade off the lamp and projected a broad shaft of light in the direction of the voice. One or two massive beams surged up, throwing austere, sharp-edged shadows, but apart from that all that could be seen was a cone of swirling dust.

Meanwhile the footsteps came closer, more confident now.

Then a foot stumbled over a plank again, even closer this time, and the next moment, pale and ashen in the shadows, Basini's face appeared at the base of the cone of light.

He was smiling – a sweet, affectionate smile. It was a fixed expression, rather like in a portrait, and set off by the frame of lamplight.

Törless pressed himself back against the crossbeam; he could feel the muscles in his eyes twitching.

In a severe, unwavering voice, Beineberg listed Basini's unspeakable deeds, and then asked him, "So aren't you ashamed of yourself?"

The look that Basini gave Reiting seemed to say: "It's time you stood up for me." But at that moment Reiting punched him in the face, and he staggered backwards, tripped over a beam and fell to the ground. Beineberg and Reiting threw themselves on him.

The lamp tipped over, and the shaft of light lay at Törless's feet, inanimate.

From the different sounds he could tell they were tearing Basini's clothes off and thrashing him with something thin and whippy. All this had clearly been agreed in advance. He could hear Basini whimpering, his faint cries of pain as he begged for mercy. Eventually there was just a moan, like a stifled howl among the muffled curses and Beineberg's heavy, excited breathing.

Törless didn't move from where he was sitting. At first he felt a brutish desire to leap up and join in, but was held back by the thought that he might be too late and just get in the way. It was as if a strong hand were gripping his limbs, leaving him paralysed.

Seemingly indifferent, he kept his gaze fixed on the floor. He didn't even strain his ears to try to interpret what the noises meant, and his heartbeat returned to normal. He studied the lamplight, the puddle it created at his feet; in it glimmered balls of fluff and a horrid little spider's web. Farther away, the rays seeped between the beams and petered out in a half-light of dust and dirt.

He could have sat like this for a whole hour without noticing. He wasn't thinking about anything, and yet his mind was totally absorbed. He was observing himself – although it was as if he were staring into a void, and only catching sidelong glimpses in a vague, confused shimmering. And then from out of the haze of uncertainty, from another oblique angle and becoming gradually more visible, a desire found its way into the clearer region of his consciousness.

Something – he wasn't sure what – made him smile. But then the desire grew stronger. It tried to drag him from where he was sitting, onto his knees, onto the floor; to make him press himself against the floorboards. He could feel his eyes getting larger and larger like a fish's, while through his naked body his heart was pounding against the planks.

He was seized with a violent agitation, and had to grip the crossbeam to stop the giddy sensation forcing him downwards. His forehead was beaded with sweat, and he began to worry what all this meant.

Roused from his apathy, he listened hard to try to work out what the other three were doing in the darkness. But everything was quiet now; all he could hear was Basini sobbing as he fumbled around for his scattered clothes.

Törless found something enjoyable about this sobbing sound. A shudder ran down his spine, as if spiders were scuttling up and down it; the sensation came to rest between his shoulder blades, and tugged at his scalp with its tiny little claws. To his consternation he realized that his excitement was of a sexual nature. Thinking back, although he couldn't remember exactly when it had started, he knew it was connected with the strange desire to press himself against the floorboards. He felt ashamed; yet it was as if he had had a sudden rush of blood to the head.

Beineberg and Reiting groped their way back and sat either side of him without saying a word. Beineberg stared at the lamp.

At this very moment, Törless felt himself being dragged down again. It started with his eyes – he could tell that now – with his eyes, as if they had hypnotized his brain into a state of rigidity. It was a question of, yes, it was a... no, it was despair... something that he was all too familiar with... the wall, the garden of the patisserie, the hovels beside the road, his childhood memories... it was the same thing! The same! He glanced at Beineberg. "Can't he feel anything?" he thought. But Beineberg just leant forward to pick up the lamp. Törless held him back. "Don't you think it's like an eye?" he said, pointing at the pool of light on the floor.

"Are you trying to be poetic?"

"No. But you admit yourself that the eyes have a special purpose, don't you? That they sometimes work with a power – think of your pet theories about hypnosis – that has nothing to do with anything we learn in physics. And it's true that you can often tell more about a person from their eyes than from what they say..."

"And?"

"To me this light is like an eye. Directed towards a different world. It's as if I'm supposed to guess something, but I can't. I want to drink it down, swallow it..."

"Now you're being poetic again."

"No, I'm serious. In fact I'm at my wits' end. Just look at it and you'll feel the same: a need to roll around in this pool, to crawl on all fours into the dirtiest, dustiest corner, as if by doing so you might be able to guess..."

"My dear fellow, that's just silly sentimentality. You mustn't fill your head with such things."

And Beineberg bent down and stood the lamp back up again. Törless had a malicious feeling of satisfaction. He realized he had a sensibility for such things, one that his classmates didn't possess.

As he waited for Basini to reappear he noticed, with a secret, inner frisson, that the tiny claws were dragging at his scalp again.

He was already acutely aware that something was being reserved for him personally, something that was signalling its presence with ever-greater insistence; a sensation that was beyond the grasp of the other two, yet which clearly had great importance for his life.

What he didn't know was what this sensual excitement meant, although he remembered that it occurred every time events began to seem strange – but only to him – and that he was tormented by his inability to understand why.

He resolved to give some serious thought to this problem at the earliest opportunity. In the meantime he abandoned himself to the excitement that preceded Basini's reappearance.

By now Beineberg had set the lamp up again, and the shaft of light traced a circle in the darkness, creating what looked like an empty frame.

And then suddenly Basini's face was there again, just like the first time, wearing the same sweet, fixed smile, as if nothing had happened; except that drops of blood were tracing bright-red, worm-like trails across his upper lip, mouth and chin.

"Sit down over there!" Reiting pointed at the enormous crossbeam. Basini obeyed. Then Reiting began: "I suppose you thought you'd get off lightly, eh? You thought I'd help you? Well that's where you were wrong. What I did with you was just to find out how low you would sink."

Basini made to protest, but Reiting looked as if he might set on him again. So Basini said: "For God's sake, I'm begging you – what else could I do?"

"Be quiet!" screamed Reiting. "We've had enough of your excuses! We know all we need to know about you now, and we'll act accordingly…"

There was a brief silence. Then suddenly, in a quiet, almost kindly voice, Törless said: "So just say 'I'm a thief'."

Basini's eyes widened in fright; Beineberg smiled approvingly.

But Basini didn't reply. Beineberg jabbed him in the ribs and yelled: "Didn't you hear? You have to say that you're a thief! Say it right now!"

Again there was a short silence; and then, in a single breath and in the most expressionless voice that he could muster, Basini said quietly: "I'm a thief."

Beineberg and Reiting turned to Törless and laughed in satisfaction: "That was a good idea of yours, lad." Then they looked at Basini: "And now you have to say: 'I am a creature, a filthy, thieving creature – *your* filthy, thieving creature!'"

Without drawing breath Basini did as he was told, keeping his eyes firmly closed.

By now Törless had leant back into the darkness again. He found the whole scene thoroughly nauseating, and was ashamed for having given away his idea to the others so cheaply.

9

I T WAS DURING A MATHS LESSON that he suddenly had another idea.

During the last few days he had been paying special attention in every lesson, because he was thinking: "If this is really preparation for life as they say it is, then there ought to be at least a hint of what I'm searching for."

And, after his ruminations on the infinite, it was mathematics in particular that was on his mind.

Then it just came to him out of the blue, in the middle of the lesson. As soon as the period was over he went and sat next to Beineberg, who was the only one he could talk to about such things.

"So did you understand all that?"

"All what?"

"All that stuff about imaginary numbers?"

"Yes. It's not terribly difficult. You just have to remember that the unit of calculation is the square root of minus one."

"Exactly – but that doesn't exist. Whether it's positive or negative, when any number is squared it always gives a positive. So there can't be any real number which could be the square root of a negative."

"Absolutely right. Even so, why shouldn't we still try to use the calculation to extract a square root from a negative number? Obviously it won't give a real value, which is why we describe the result as imaginary. It's as if we're saying: someone has always sat here, so we'll put out a chair for him today as usual; and even if in the meantime he has died, we'll still behave as if he's going to come."

"But how can we do that, when we know for certain – with mathematical certainty in fact – that it's impossible?"

"That's precisely the point, we should behave as if it isn't impossible. It might prove quite successful. After all, isn't that always the case with irrational numbers? A process of division that never ends, a fraction whose true value will never ever be known, regardless of how far we take the calculation? And how do we set about visualizing the fact that two parallel lines only ever intersect at infinity? I think if we tried to be overly punctilious there wouldn't be any mathematics at all."

"I agree with you on that point. If you view it from that angle then it certainly does seems odd. But what's even more peculiar is that we can still use imaginary or impossible values to perform real calculations and get a tangible result!"

"It's simply that for those purposes, the imaginary factors cancel each other out during the course of the calculation."

"Yes yes, I know that as well as you do. But isn't there still something extremely odd about the whole thing? How can I put it? Think of it like this: at the start of any calculation of this kind there are always concrete figures which represent length or weight or something tangible, and which are at least real. And at the end of the calculation there is something similar.

But these two sets of figures are connected by something that doesn't exist. Isn't it like a bridge that only has supports at each end, and yet we still walk across quite happily as if the whole construction were intact? Calculations like that make my head spin; as if at one point the road leads God knows where. But to me the most mysterious thing is the hidden power contained in calculations like that, which hold on to you so tightly that you arrive safely on the other side."

Beineberg grinned: "Now you're beginning to sound like our parish priest. 'You see an apple – there are waves of oscillating light, your eyes, et cetera – and you reach out your hand to steal it – there are nerves and muscles which cause these to move – but between these things there is something else, which makes them happen in sequence, and that is your immortal soul, which by doing this has committed a sin... Oh yes, yes! None of your actions can be explained without the soul, which plays you like the keys of a piano...'" And he imitated the voice of the catechist repeating the age-old, traditional comparison. "But none of that really interests me."

"Well I think it ought to interest you. At least, it made me think of you straight away, because if it's really so inexplicable then it would confirm your beliefs."

"Why shouldn't it be inexplicable? I find it perfectly possible that the people who invented mathematics simply tripped over their own feet. Why shouldn't something that is beyond our powers of understanding not play tricks on us? But I don't concern myself with such things, they never lead anywhere."

10

THAT SAME DAY, Törless asked the maths tutor if he could come and see him to get him to explain some of the lesson in more detail.

The next day during lunch break he walked up the stairs to the master's small set of rooms.

He had acquired a new respect for mathematics, which had changed from being a dry-as-dust subject that he was forced to study into something very much about life. Along with this respect he felt a certain envy for the master, who was undoubtedly familiar with this field and carried his knowledge around with him like the key to a secret garden. He was also driven by a hesitant curiosity. He had never been in a young man's room before, and was itching to find out how this learned but reserved individual lived, or at least as far as he was able to judge from the objects with which he surrounded himself.

Törless was generally shy and unforthcoming with the masters, and so had no reason to believe that this one felt particularly well disposed towards him. Now he was standing nervously outside the door, his request seemed an act of daring that would not so much help him to get some explanations – which deep down he already doubted he would receive – as to catch a glimpse, over his tutor's shoulder so to speak, of the man's everyday cohabitation with the art of mathematics.

He was shown into the study. It was a long room with only one window, beside which stood an ink-stained desk, and, against the wall, a sofa upholstered in coarse green corded fabric decorated with tassels. Above it hung a faded undergraduate's cap and an assortment of yellowing, post-card-sized photographs taken during his time at university. On the oval table, which had X-shaped feet, and whose spiral scrolls attempted to give an impression of grace and elegance but just looked like a misplaced curtsey, lay a pipe and some cheap, rough-cut tobacco. The smell of it filled the entire room.

Törless barely had time to absorb these impressions and to register a certain feeling of discontent, as if a dish of unappetizing food had just been put in front of him, before the master walked in.

He was quite young, no more than thirty, fair-haired and quite highly strung: a very capable mathematician who had already given a number of noteworthy papers at the Academy.

He immediately went over and sat at the desk, rummaged around for a moment among the papers that were lying all over it (only later did it occur to Törless that he had gone straight there to seek refuge), cleaned his pince-nez with his handkerchief, crossed his legs and then turned to Törless with a look of expectation.

Having studied the room, Törless now began to scrutinize his tutor. He noticed the thick, white woollen socks, and that the under-straps of his fitted trousers were scuffed black by boot polish where they fastened under his shoes.

His handkerchief, on the other hand, was brilliant white and prettily embroidered, and although his cravat had been mended in places it was as gaily coloured as a painter's palette.

Törless couldn't help feeling even more put off by these observations: there was little hope that the man possessed any significant knowledge, as there was nothing about him or his surroundings that suggested he might. He had imagined a mathematician's study quite differently: there would be evidence of the terrifying thoughts that came into being here. Its banality offended him, and so he transferred this feeling onto mathematics itself, and his newfound respect began to give way to mistrust and hesitation.

As the maths tutor shifted impatiently in his chair, not knowing quite what to make of this prolonged silence or the boy's penetrating gaze, an atmosphere of misunderstanding began to take hold between them.

"Well then… we could… you could… I'm perfectly happy to answer any questions you might have," the young man began.

Törless told him what his objections were, and did his best to explain the sense in which he understood them. But he felt as if he were speaking through dense, swirling mist, and that his best arguments were sticking in his throat.

The master smiled, coughed, and then said: "Do you mind if I smoke?", lit a cigarette and took rapid little drags at it; the paper – details which in the meantime Törless had noted and found utterly mundane – was soon stained with grease and crackled with every puff. The man took off his pince-nez, put them back on again, nodded... but in the end he didn't even let Törless finish what he was saying. "I'm delighted, my dear Törless, absolutely delighted," he said, interrupting him. "Your misgivings are a sign of seriousness, of mature reflection, of... hmm... but it isn't easy to give you the explanation you're looking for... please don't misunderstand me on this point.

"Let me see, you were talking about the role of transcendent... hmm, yes, that's the name usually given to them... transcendent factors...

"Of course it's true that I'm not privy to your feelings on the matter; questions of a super-sensory nature, which go beyond the defined boundaries of reason, are a quite specialized subject. I'm not really qualified to comment, as it lies outside my field; people have different opinions about it, and I certainly wouldn't want to inveigh against anyone... But as far as mathematics is concerned" – and he stressed the word "mathematics" as if he were closing a door behind him, inevitably and for all time – "as far as mathematics itself is concerned, it's clear that what we are dealing with here is a natural and purely mathematical relationship.

"But from a strictly scientific viewpoint, I would first have to go over certain basic assumptions that you might find hard to understand, and in any case we don't have time.

"Please don't misunderstand me, I appreciate that concepts such as imaginary numerical values for example, which don't actually exist, are a hard nut for younger minds to crack, ha ha. You must content yourself with the fact that such concepts necessarily belong to the domain of pure mathematics. Think of it like this: at the elementary level where you are at present, we can only touch on many questions that would be difficult to explain in sufficient detail. Fortunately, very few pupils realize this, but when one of them comes along, as you have today – and as I said, I'm delighted that you did – then all one can say is this: you simply have to believe it, my friend, simply believe. When you know ten times more about mathematics than you do now, then you will understand – but in the meantime, believe!

"There's nothing else one can do, my dear Törless. Mathematics is a world unto itself, and one has to have lived in it for a very long time to acquire the necessary knowledge."

Törless was glad when the master stopped talking. Ever since he heard the fateful door closing it had seemed as if the words were drifting farther and farther away... towards that other shore, the one where nothing mattered, where all the correct but unimportant explanations were kept.

He was so dazed by the torrent of words and the sense of having failed that at first he didn't realize that it was time for him to go.

So in order to settle the matter, the maths tutor decided to try one last conclusive argument.

On a small side table, somewhat ostentatiously, as if it were a showpiece, was a volume of Kant. The master picked it up and showed it to Törless. "See this book? This is philosophy: it deals with the factors that determine our behaviour. If you were to succeed in sounding its depths you would be confronted with even more of these necessary axioms that determine everything – although without further study they remain incomprehensible. It's much the same with mathematics. And yet we continually act according to these axioms – which proves just how important they are. But" – and he smiled as he saw Törless open the book and immediately start flicking through it – "leave that for now. I just wanted to give you an example that you would remember and come back to later: for the time being it would probably be too difficult for you."

Törless spent the rest of the day in a state of turmoil.

The fact of having laid hands on a volume of Kant – a chance event that he paid scant attention to at the time – had a profound effect on him. He had certainly heard Kant's name and, as a result of mixing with people who were only vaguely concerned with intellectual matters, he was aware of his standing as the last word in philosophy. This aura of authority was one of the reasons he tended to avoid works of a serious nature. Once they have outgrown the phase when they want to be a coachman, a gardener or run a sweetshop, young people generally begin to harbour ambitions of carving out a career in those areas where they imagine they will have the greatest opportunities to distinguish themselves. So when they say they want to be a doctor, one can be sure that somewhere they have seen a delightful waiting room full of patients, or a showcase of mysterious surgical instruments or something similar; if they talk of entering the diplomatic service, what they have in mind is the glamour and elegance of international receptions: in a nutshell, they choose their occupation according to the milieu where they prefer to see themselves, the pose they find most appealing.

Törless had only ever heard Kant's name mentioned in passing, by people whose expression suggested they were referring to a fearsome deity. So it was inevitable that he should believe that Kant had solved philosophy's problems once and for all, and that it was now a futile occupation, in the same way as he thought that after Goethe and Schiller there was little point in writing verse.

At home these books were kept in Papa's study, in a bookcase with green glass doors, and he knew it was only ever opened to show visitors. It was like the shrine of some divine being whom we are loath to approach, and whom we only worship because its existence relieves us of the need to worry about such things.

Later on, this distorted relationship with philosophy and literature had a regrettable influence on Törless's intellectual development, and caused him a deal of unhappiness. At the very moment when his ambition, diverted from its proper objectives, was in search of a new aim to replace the one it had been deprived of, it came under the brutal and determined influence of his classmates. His true inclinations only reappeared occasionally and with diffidence, and always left him with the feeling of having done something pointless and absurd. Yet so powerful were they that he could never quite succeed in freeing himself from them, and it was this endless struggle that prevented his character from taking shape and developing along solid lines.

Today, however, this relationship seemed to have entered a new phase. The ideas for which he had vainly sought an explanation were no longer just random, unconnected games played by his imagination, they now churned him over and over and refused to let go, and he sensed with his whole being that behind them another part of his life was pounding with its fists to be released. All this was new to him. Deep down inside him there was a firmness that he had never known before. It was mysterious, almost dream-like. It had probably grown in silent seclusion under the influence of recent events, and was now drumming its fingers imperiously. He was like a mother who feels the tyrannical stirrings of her unborn child inside her for the first time.

It was a wonderfully elating afternoon.

He went to his locker and took out all the attempts at poetry that he kept there. Then he sat by himself beside the stove, hidden behind the tall, heavy screen. One by one he flicked through the exercise books, then slowly tore them to pieces and threw them into the fire, savouring the delicate sensation of parting every time.

His motive for doing this was to rid himself of his old, unwanted baggage, as if from now on – unencumbered – he would concentrate his attention on the steps that would carry him forward.

When he had finished he went back and joined the rest of the class. He now felt free of all the anxious sidelong glances. Yet what he had done was purely instinctive: the only thing that could reassure him that from now on he would be a new person was the mere fact of this impulse. "Tomorrow," he told himself, "tomorrow I'll reassess everything carefully, and then I'll definitely find some clarity."

He strolled round the classroom, between the desks, glancing at the open exercise books across whose dazzling-white pages fingers were busily writing, each casting its small brown shadow behind it; he watched them like someone who has suddenly woken up, and to whom everything seems to have taken on much greater significance.

11

B UT THE NEXT DAY brought bitter disappointment. In the morning he bought himself a popular edition of the great volume that he had seen in the maths master's study, and set about reading it during the first break. But what with all the brackets and footnotes he didn't understand a word, and as his eyes dutifully followed the phrases it felt as if an old, bony hand was gradually unscrewing his brain from inside his head.

When after half an hour he stopped, exhausted, he had got no further than the second page, and his forehead was covered in sweat.

Gritting his teeth he managed to read another page before the end of break.

That evening, however, he couldn't bring himself even to touch the book. Was it fear or revulsion? He wasn't sure. There was only one question that consumed him – that the maths master, pitiful little man that he was, had this book lying around open in his study as if it were an everyday pastime for him.

It was in this frame of mind that he bumped into Beineberg.

"So how did it go with the maths tutor yesterday, Törless?" They sat in a window alcove and pulled a coat rack full of overcoats in front of them, so that all that reached them from the classroom was an intermittent humming noise and the reflection of the lamps on the ceiling. Törless fiddled absentmindedly with the coats.

"Are you still asleep or something? He must have given you some kind of answer, didn't he? Mind you, I can imagine that he was ever so slightly flustered!"

"Why?"

"Because he wasn't expecting such a stupid question – that's why."

"It wasn't a stupid question: in fact, I can't get it out of my mind."

"I didn't mean it like that – just that it must have seemed stupid to him. They all learn their subject off by heart like a priest does the catechism, but as soon as someone asks them something slightly off-script they get flustered."

"Well he certainly wasn't flustered when it came to an answer. He had one ready and waiting, he didn't even let me finish what I was saying."

"And so how did he explain everything?"

"He didn't, actually. He just told me I wasn't in a position to understand it yet, that they were axioms that only become clearer to those who have studied them in depth."

"That's just the same old con! They're incapable of explaining this stuff to people whose minds aren't fully trained. It only works when someone's had it hammered into him for ten years. By then he's done thousands of calculations based on those principles, and constructed vast great edifices that will hold until the end of time; by that point he believes in his subject like a Catholic believes in the Revelation, it has always amply proved its worth... so it doesn't take much skill to talk someone like that into believing the evidence, does it? Quite the reverse: no one would be able to convince him that even if this edifice of his were still standing, if someone wanted to take away any of the bricks it's built with then it would just vanish into thin air!"

Törless didn't much like Beineberg's exaggerations.

"I don't think you need to go quite as far as that. I've never doubted that what mathematics claims is true – after all, its results are living proof – although one thing I do find odd is how it sometimes seems to go against all reason – but on the other hand that might only be the way it seems."

"You'll just have to wait for ten years, and then perhaps your mind will be properly trained... But since the last time we discussed this I've been thinking about it too, and I'm absolutely convinced there's a catch somewhere. In any case, you were talking quite differently the other day."

"No, I wasn't. It's true that I still have doubts, but I don't want to immediately start exaggerating like you do. I find the whole thing *bizarre* as well. Whenever I try to imagine the irrational, the imaginary, parallel lines that intersect at the point of infinity – or somewhere else – it makes me nervous. Just thinking about it leaves me in a daze, as if I've had a blow to the head." Törless leant forward in the shadows, and his voice became slightly husky. "Everything used to be so clear, so neat and tidy in my mind; but now my thoughts are like clouds, and there are places between them like gaps through which I can see a sort of limitless, indeterminate expanse. There's no doubt that mathematics is correct – but what about inside my head, other people's heads? Can't they feel anything? How do they picture it? Don't they imagine anything at all?"

"I think you can see the answer to that in your maths tutor. But whenever you come up against something like this, your immediate reaction is to look round and wonder how it fits with everything else within you. Whereas *they* have bored a long, spiralling tunnel deep into their brains, and just keep glancing back to make sure that the thread they have spun behind them hasn't snapped at the last bend. Which is why the sort of question you asked always leaves them nonplussed. It makes them lose their way. And how can you say I'm exaggerating, by the way? All these grown men, these great thinkers, have spun a web around themselves in which each link supports the next one, so the whole miraculous construction looks perfectly natural; yet where the original link is hidden, the one that holds all the rest together, no one knows.

"You and I have never talked about this quite so seriously before, but then people don't like getting involved in discussions about things of this kind, and you can see now how content they are to have these pitiful opinions about the world. It's nothing but a delusion, a con, feeble-mindedness! Anaemia! Their brains stretch just far enough for them to work out their learned little theory, but the moment it gets beyond the scope of their thinking it freezes to death, do you see what I mean? Oh yes! All these soaring peaks, these fine points that the masters say are too lofty for us to reach, they're all dead – frozen – do you understand? All around us are icy peaks that we gaze at admiringly, but no one even begins to know what to do with them, they're so utterly lifeless!"

For some time Törless had been sitting back against the window. Beineberg's warm breath was trapped among the coats, heating up the little corner where they were sitting. As always when he got excited he had an unpleasant effect on Törless; especially now he was leaning forward, so close that his staring eyes were right in front of Törless like a pair of greenish-coloured stones, while his hands twitched about in the shadows in a particularly repulsive, agitated way.

"None of their claims are proven. Everything happens according to nature's laws, or so they say. When a stone falls it's due to gravity, so why shouldn't it be God's will, and why shouldn't someone who is pleasing to God be spared the same fate as the stone? But what's the point of talking to you about these things? You'll never get any further than halfway! You'll uncover one or two oddities, you'll shake your head for a moment, be vaguely horrified – that's the way you are. You daren't go any further. But it's no loss to me."

"And so is it my loss? Your own claims aren't exactly proven either."

"How can you say that? They're the only ones that are proven, actually. But there's no reason to quarrel! You'll understand eventually, my dear Törless; I'd even be prepared to wager that one day you'll develop a hell of an interest in this question. For example, if everything goes according to plan with Basini, like I—"

"Just drop it, will you?" Törless interrupted. "I'd rather not get involved with that at the moment."

"Oh? And why not?"

"Because. I just don't want to, that's why. I find it unpleasant. As far as I'm concerned, Basini and this are two completely separate matters, and I'm not in the habit of lumping everything in the same basket."

Confronted with this uncharacteristic assurance, even rudeness from the younger boy, Beineberg pulled an angry face. Yet Törless had the feeling that the very mention of Basini's name would undermine his self-confidence, and so to conceal this he too responded angrily: "And anyway, you make these claims with a certainty that's completely insane. Has it never occurred to you that your own theories might be just as much built on sand as all the rest? They're an even more tortuous labyrinth, and demand even more good faith in order to believe them."

Curiously enough, Beineberg wasn't annoyed: he just smiled – albeit a somewhat strained smile, while his eyes glinted even more feverishly than before – and repeated: "You'll see, you'll definitely see…"

"What will I see? Fine, if you say so then I'll see – but I don't give a fig, Beineberg! You don't understand. You haven't the faintest idea what interests me. If I'm struggling with mathematics and if I…" – but he quickly changed his mind and decided not to mention Basini – "if I'm struggling with mathematics it's because I'm looking for something completely different from you, nothing remotely supernatural; on the contrary, what I'm searching for is perfectly natural – don't you understand? It's not anything outside me, but inside me, inside! Something natural! Although it's something I don't understand! But you have no more feeling for it than you do for mathematics… oh, do stop bothering me with all your speculation, will you!"

When he stood up, Törless was quivering with agitation.

But Beineberg just kept repeating: "We'll see, oh yes, we'll see…"

12

TÖRLESS COULDN'T GET TO SLEEP that night. As he lay there, the quarter-hours came round like a constant relay of nurses hovering at his bedside. His feet were like blocks of ice, and instead of keeping him warm the blankets seemed to be smothering him.

All that could be heard in the dormitory was the soft, regular breathing of the other boys who, after a day of lessons, gymnastics and running around in the fresh air had fallen into a deep, animal sleep.

He listened to the sound of sleeping. It might be Beineberg's breathing, or Reiting's, or Basini's. Whose was it? He couldn't tell; he just knew they were all part of this calm, confident, regular sound which rose and fell like the workings of a well-oiled machine.

One of the canvas window blinds had only been pulled halfway down; through the gap beneath it the bright, clear moonlight threw a pale, motionless rectangle onto the floor. The cord must have got caught at the top or had come off its pulley, and hung down in hideous coils, its shadow slithering across the rectangle of light on the floor like a worm.

All these details were horrifyingly, monstrously ugly.

He tried to think of something pleasant. Beineberg came to mind. Hadn't he outmanoeuvred him? Dented his sense of superiority? Hadn't he managed to protect his individuality from the others for once? To emphasize how infinitely superior his delicate sensitivities were, how they set him apart from their concept of the world? So had he had the last word? Yes or no?…

But this "yes or no" swelled up in his head like so many bubbles which then burst, and – yes or no, yes or no – kept growing and growing like the pounding rhythm of an express train, like flowers nodding their heads at the top of tall stems, like the banging of a hammer that can be heard through the thin walls of a silent house... This overpowering, self-satisfied "yes or no" turned his stomach. It was absurd how his delight was hopping and skipping around in this way; it couldn't be genuine.

When he woke with a start, it felt as if his own head was nodding, lolling about on his shoulders, tapping out a beat like a hammer...

Eventually everything fell silent inside him. There was just an enormous black expanse before him, spreading in ever-growing circles in all directions.

And then... from the farthest edge of this expanse... two tiny figures came tottering diagonally across the table. He could see quite clearly that it was his parents; but they were so small that he was unable to have any feelings for them.

When they got to the other side they vanished.

Then two more figures appeared – but what was this? A third one came running up from behind and overtook them with great strides that were twice as long as his body; in fact he had disappeared over the edge of the table already. Wasn't it Beineberg? And the other two? Wasn't one of them the maths master? Törless recognized him from the little handkerchief peeping playfully from his top pocket. But what about the other one? Under his arm he had an extremely thick book almost as big as he was, and which he was barely able to drag along. With every other step he stopped and put it down. And then Törless heard his maths tutor's squeaky voice: "If I'm not mistaken we should find the answer on page twelve, and page twelve will refer us to page fifty-two, but we should also take account of the note on page thirty-one, and on this assumption..." They stood hunched over the book, manhandling the pages so energetically that clouds of dust rose from them. After a while they stood up again, and the other figure stroked the master's cheek five or six times. Then they took a few steps forward, and again Törless heard the voice, exactly the same as in maths lessons when it embarked on a long, tapeworm-like theorem; on and on until the other person began to stroke the master's cheek again.

The other person... Törless peered, trying to see him more clearly. Wasn't he wearing a powdered wig? Rather old-fashioned clothes? Extremely old-fashioned in fact. And even silk knee breeches? Wasn't it?... Oh yes! Törless woke with a start and exclaimed: "Kant!"

Then he smiled. All around him the dormitory was quiet and still, the sound of breathing much less audible. In the meantime he had been asleep too, and his bed was warmer. He stretched out contentedly beneath the covers.

"So I dreamt about Kant," he thought. "Why didn't it last longer? We could have had a chat, he might have let something slip." And he remembered once, when he hadn't done his history prep, how the night before the lesson he had had a dream about the people and events in question which was so vivid that the next day he was able to talk about them as if he had been there in person, and got an A on the test. And then suddenly he remembered Beineberg, Beineberg and Kant – the conversation they had had the day before.

Gradually the dream receded, like a silk sheet slipping slowly, gently, endlessly off a naked body.

But his smile soon gave way to a strange sense of disquiet. Had he really got any further forward with his reflections? Was he able to draw *any* conclusions from this book, which was supposed to contain the solution to every enigma in the world? And his victory? It was probably just his unexpected brusqueness that had left Beineberg speechless.

Again he was filled with a profound listlessness, an actual, physical desire to vomit. For a few minutes he lay there, drained by feelings of nausea.

Then once again he became conscious of the soft, warm sensation of the sheets touching every part of his body. Slowly and very, very carefully he turned his head. Yes, the pale rectangle was still there on the stone floor, and although it was now slightly distorted the sinuous shadow was still creeping across it. It seemed as if there was something dangerous chained up over there that he could keep watch on from the safety of his bed as if he were protected by iron bars, serene in the knowledge that he was out of harm's way.

All of a sudden, in his skin, all over the surface of his body, he began to get a feeling that soon became a memory. When he was very young – yes, that was it – when he still wore dresses and didn't yet go to school, there were times when he had an indescribable longing to be a little girl. Yet this longing wasn't in his head – oh no! – nor did it come from his heart: it was more like a tickling sensation all over his body, an irritation beneath the skin. Yes, there were moments when he felt so vividly that he was a little girl that he believed it must be true. At the time, of course, he had no idea what physical differences meant, and couldn't understand why everyone around him was always telling him that he would have to be a boy for ever. And whenever someone asked him why he thought he was a girl, he sensed that it wasn't something that could be explained...

Now today, for the first time he had a similar sensation. And once again it was just beneath his skin.

It was something that seemed both physical and psychological at once. As if thousands of velvety butterflies' antennae were chasing their way across his body. And at the same time it had that air of defiance with which young girls suddenly rush off when they sense that adults simply won't understand them, that arrogance with which they giggle at them behind their backs, that timid arrogance that is always ready to run away and tells them that they can withdraw into some oh-so-secret hiding place inside their little bodies at any moment...

He laughed quietly to himself, and stretched out contentedly beneath the covers again.

That funny little man in his dream, how voraciously his fingers had turned the pages of the book! And what about that rectangle on the floor? What of it! As if such clever little men had ever noticed anything like that in their entire lives! He felt perfectly secure from these clever individuals, and for the first time he realized that in his sensual nature – and he had known this for some time – he possessed something that no one could take away from him or imitate, something that protected him from any strange, foreign intelligence like a high, hidden wall.

So had these clever little men ever lain at the foot of a secluded wall, he wondered, pursuing the idea further, had they ever been alarmed at the merest quiver beneath its surface, as if some long-dead presence inside it were trying to find the right words with which to communicate with them? Had they ever felt the music that the wind whips up among the autumn leaves – experienced it deeply and profoundly enough so that, lurking behind it, they suddenly discovered a horror that slowly and gradually turns into sensual pleasure? Yet a sensual pleasure so strange that it is more like an escape, and then a mocking laugh. Oh yes, it was easy to be clever when you were unaware of all these problems...

In the meantime, however, the funny little man seemed to be growing bigger and bigger until he became enormous, with an implacably severe expression on his face, and every time Törless looked at him something like a painful electric shock shot from his brain all the way through his body. It was the pain of being forced to stand outside a closed door, a pain which a few moments before had been thrust aside by the warm pulsing of his blood, and which now came back to him, and a wordless lament surged through his soul like the tremulous howling of a dog echoing across the open fields at night.

With that he fell asleep again. Once or twice as he was drifting off he glanced at the patch of light under the window, in the way we instinctively pull at a safety rope to make sure it is still taut. And then the vague intention began to take shape that tomorrow he would have to give this some careful thought, preferably with pen and paper at hand, yet in the end there was just the deliciously warm sensation – like a bath or sensual experience – that didn't come to him in isolation, but which in some obscure yet powerful way was associated with Basini.

Then he fell into a deep, dreamless sleep.

13

YET THIS WAS THE FIRST THING that came to him when he woke the next morning. He would have dearly loved to know exactly what he had begun to think and dream about Basini as he was falling asleep, but he couldn't remember.

All that remained was a trace of the gentle, affectionate atmosphere that reigns in a house before Christmas, when the children know that the presents are there, but hidden away behind the mysterious locked door, through which filters only the occasional chink of light.

At the end of school that evening he stayed behind in the classroom. Beineberg and Reiting had disappeared somewhere, probably up to the room in the attic; Basini was sitting in his usual place at the front, head in his hands and studying a book.

Törless had bought an exercise book, and carefully laid out pen and ink beside it. After a moment's hesitation he wrote at the top of the first page: "*De natura hominum*", as he felt that such a philosophical subject was worthy of a Latin title.

Finally he drew a large, elaborate scroll around the heading and then sat back to wait for the ink to dry.

But even after it had been dry for some time, he still hadn't picked up his pen. Something was holding him back. It was the entrancing atmosphere created by the blazing gas lamps, the animal warmth generated by a room full of bodies. He had always been susceptible to this environment, which was capable of making him quite feverish, and was invariably accompanied by an extraordinary level of intellectual and spiritual acuity. As was the case now. All day he had been mentally preparing himself for what he was going to write about: the whole series of experiences since the evening with Božena up until the last few days, when this ill-defined fit of sensuality had set in. Once everything was arranged in order, labelled fact by fact, then he hoped that the true, rational workings of his mind would appear of their own volition, in the way a shape emerges from the wild confusion of hundreds of intersecting curves. He asked for no more than that. Yet up till now he had been like a fisherman who feels a tug on the line and thinks he has a good catch in the net, but despite his best efforts isn't able to haul it into the boat.

Nonetheless he began to write, albeit hurriedly and with scant regard for what form it might take. "I can sense something within me," he noted, "and I'm not sure what it is." But he immediately crossed this out and replaced it with: "I think I must be ill… even mad!" And a shudder ran through him, so deliciously dramatic did it sound. "Mad – because otherwise why am I alarmed by things that other people find perfectly normal? And tormented by this alarm? Why does it make me feel so shameless?" He chose this last word, with its overtones of biblical unction, quite intentionally, because he found it more obscure, richer in meaning. "Up till now I've had the same attitudes as other boys of my age, as all my classmates…" Here he broke off, however. "But is that really true?" he thought. "With Božena, for example, it was actually quite bizarre; so when exactly did it start?… Still, it doesn't matter," he thought, "it just started." Yet he left the sentence unfinished.

"What are the things that alarm me? The most insignificant ones. Mostly inanimate objects. What is it about them that alarms me? Something I don't recognize. But that's just the point! Where does this 'something' come from? I can sense its presence; it has an effect on me; it's as if it wants to talk to me. I'm as agitated as someone who is trying to read the contorted lips of a paralysed man, but with no success. It's as if I have an extra sense that other people don't have, a sense that is there, which draws attention to itself, yet which doesn't function. For me the world is full of mute voices: so am I a visionary, or am I hallucinating?

"But it isn't just inanimate objects that have this effect on me – no, what also troubles me is human beings. Up to a certain point in time I used to see them as they see themselves. Beineberg and Reiting for instance – they have their little room, an ordinary room in the attic, because it amuses them to have a retreat where they can go and hide. They do one thing because they are angry with a certain individual, and another because they want to prevent that individual from influencing their friend. All perfectly clear, comprehensible motives. But sometimes it seems as if I'm dreaming, and that they are part of that dream. Not just what they say, not just what they do – no, everything about them, everything associated with their physical proximity has an effect on me, in the same way inanimate objects do. And yet I can still hear them talking just like before, everything they do and say follows exactly the same unchanging form… as if to continually reassure me that nothing out of the ordinary is happening, while equally continually something inside me contradicts this. If I remember correctly, these changes began when Basini…"

And before he knew what he was doing, he had glanced in his direction.

Basini was still staring at his book, and appeared to be doing his prep. Seeing him sitting there, Törless's mind emptied of thoughts, and he could feel the same delicious torments that he had just been describing beginning to take effect on him again. And as soon as he saw how quiet and inoffensive Basini was, sitting there in the front row, how he was no different from the boys either side of him, then the humiliations that Basini had endured came alive for him. He actually relived them: which is not to say that he believed – as those of a moral disposition might be inclined to do, with that joviality peculiar to them – that after suffering a humiliation everyone tries to regain at least an outward appearance of composure and normality; instead, a wild swirling was unleashed inside him, taking the image of Basini and disfiguring it into the most unbelievable, impossible contortions, to the point where it made him dizzy. Admittedly these were only comparisons that he made later on. At the time he just had the impression that an incredible spinning top was whirling its way up from his contracting chest to his head, the centre of his giddiness. Among all the confusion, like splashes of colour, were scattered the emotions that he had felt for Basini at different times.

In reality there had only ever been one emotion. To be precise, it was not so much a feeling as a tremor deep below the surface, whose waves were not visible above ground, and which shook his soul so violently and yet with such restraint that the waves of the most tempestuous emotions seemed like ripples on a millpond by comparison.

If he only became aware of this emotion in different forms and at different times, it was because his only means of understanding the wave that washed over his being were the images captured by his senses, in the way that flecks of foam shoot up momentarily from the great swell rolling endlessly into the darkness, spraying over the rocks of a sunlit shore only to drop back immediately outside the circle of light.

As a result his impressions were erratic, changeable and accompanied by an awareness of their transitory nature. Not once was he able to retain them, for no sooner did he fix his gaze on them than he realized that these emissaries at the surface bore little relationship to the power of the dark, unfathomable mass that they claimed to represent.

Not once did he actually "see" Basini as a distinct and lively physical presence in any particular pose; in fact he had no vision of him at all. It was simply an illusion, in a sense just a vision of his visions. It always seemed as if an image had just flashed across a vast, mysterious expanse, and he was never able to catch hold of it at the moment it appeared. This was why he was in a state of constant agitation, not dissimilar to what we sometimes experience at the cinema, when, along with the illusion created by the whole film, we can never quite shake off the vague awareness that behind the images we actually see countless others are flashing past, each one, when viewed individually, quite different from the rest.

Yet exactly where within himself he might find this power of illusion – which was always too weak to create a true illusion – he didn't know. He just had a vague inkling about his relationship with his soul's mysterious ability to detect thousands of silent, questioning gazes in ordinary inanimate objects.

So there he sat, motionless, unable to take his eyes off Basini, totally caught up in this state of inner turmoil. From its depths the same question kept resurfacing again and again: "What exactly is this special quality that I have?" Gradually he lost sight of Basini and the blazing gas lamps, he no longer felt the animal warmth that hung in the air around him, the murmuring and humming that comes from a crowd of people even if they are only whispering. It swirled around him in a hot, dark, confused mass. All he could feel was that his ears were burning and the tips of his fingers were like ice. He recognized it, not as a bodily fever but the fever of the soul that he so adored. It grew stronger and stronger, mingled with tender emotions. Whenever he had found himself in this state in the past he had enjoyed abandoning himself to the memories that are left behind in a young soul after a woman's warm breath has brushed against it for the first time. That same weary warmth was now reawakened in him. He remembered... It was during a trip to... a small town in Italy... he and his parents were staying at a hotel not far from the theatre. Every evening they performed the same opera, and every evening he heard every word, every note. But he couldn't understand much of the language. And yet every evening he sat by the open window and listened. Thus it was that he fell in love with one of the actresses without ever setting eyes on her. Never had he been so overwhelmed by the theatre; in the passion of the arias he felt the beating wings of a great dark bird, it was as if he could follow the trace of their flight into the depths of his soul. It was no longer human passions he heard, but passions that had escaped from human hearts as if from a cramped, prosaic cage. In this state of excitement he was incapable of thinking about the people who – unseen – were acting out these passions somewhere nearby; if he tried to imagine them, dark flames would shoot up in front of his eyes, or incredible gigantic forms, as if human bodies were growing in the shadows, their eyes shining as if reflected in the depths of a well. At the time it was this sombre flame, these eyes in the darkness, these black, beating wings that he loved under the name of an unknown opera singer.

Who had written the opera? He didn't know. Perhaps the libretto was taken from an insipid romantic novel. Thanks to this music, had its author sensed it becoming something entirely different?

A sudden thought made his whole body contract. So was it the same for adults? For the whole world? Was there some universal law that decreed that there was something within us that is stronger, bigger, finer, darker and more passionate than ourselves? Something over which we have so little control that all we can do is scatter thousands of seeds at random, until suddenly a plant shoots up like a dark, sombre flame and soon grows taller than we are?... And from every fibre of his being came the impatient answer: "Yes."

Eyes shining, he looked round the room. The gas lamps, the warmth, the light, the industrious schoolboys were still there. And it occurred to him that among all of them he was the chosen one, like a saint blessed with celestial visions... for as yet he knew nothing of the intuition of great artists.

Quickly, with almost fearful haste, he picked up his pen and jotted down a few notes about his discovery; again it seemed as if a light were blazing brightly inside him, shining out across vast open spaces... and then an ash-grey rain began to fall on his eyes, and the many-coloured glare that had been dazzling him from within faded and disappeared.

By now he had virtually put the Kant interlude behind him; during the day he never gave it a thought. The conviction that he was on the verge of finding the answer to the enigma was too strong for him to worry about someone else's methods. Ever since the previous evening he had had the impression that he had gripped the handle of the door that led to the beyond, but it had slipped from his grasp. Yet having realized that he would have to do without the help of philosophy, and as he had little confidence in it anyway, he just stood where he was, at a loss to know how he could find this door again. He made a few sporadic attempts to carry on with his notes, but everything he wrote lay lifeless on the page, a series of sullen, all too familiar question marks, without a single repetition of that moment when through the lines he had caught a glimpse of what looked like a great vault lit up by trembling candle flames.

So he decided that, as often as possible, he would make a point of seeking out situations that had this special significance for him; and his gaze would often settle on Basini, particularly when he thought no one was watching him as he moved quite innocently among all the others. "One day," Törless thought to himself, "it will come alive again, perhaps even more clearly and vividly than before." And when it came to questions of this kind he was comforted by the thought that a person might find himself in a darkened room, where, if he couldn't discover the way out, there would be nothing to do except feel his way round the dark walls with his fingers on the off-chance that he might stumble across it.

At night, however, these thoughts lost some of their intensity. He felt a certain shame for having shied away from his original intention, which was to try to find an explanation in the book that his maths tutor had shown him, and which may have contained one. He lay there in silence, listening to Basini's breathing, this defiled body that was sleeping as peacefully as all the rest. He lay perfectly still, like a hunter in his hide, with the feeling that his long wait would eventually be rewarded. But no sooner had the idea of the book reappeared than a sharp, nagging doubt began to gnaw away at his peace of mind, along with the suspicion that he was wasting his time, and what was almost an admission of defeat.

As soon as this vague sensation made its presence felt he lost the sense of satisfaction with which we stand back and observe the progress of a scientific experiment. It was as if Basini were exerting a physical influence, the kind of temptation we feel when a woman is lying asleep beside us and we can draw back the covers whenever we choose: a tickling in the brain that comes from the knowledge that all we have to do is reach out our hand... The same thing that drives young couples to excesses that go far beyond their sexual needs.

Depending on how clear it was to him that this undertaking might seem absurd if he knew everything that Kant, his maths tutor or anyone else who had finished their education knew, or on how violently he was shaken by this idea, the sensual impulses that kept his eyes wide open and burning despite the silence and sleep all around him either grew stronger or died down. There were moments when they blazed so brightly that all other thoughts were suppressed. If he surrendered half-willingly, half-despairingly to their suggestions he was no different from the majority of people who have never indulged in such a wild, orgiastic and soul-wrenching fit of sensuality, except when their self-confidence is shattered by a defeat.

Once or twice around midnight, when he finally drifted off into a fitful sleep, he thought he saw someone get up in the vague area of Reiting's or Beineberg's bed, fetch a coat and walk over to where Basini slept. Then they left the dormitory together... but it might just have been his imagination.

14

NOT LONG AFTERWARDS there were two days' holiday, and as these fell on a Monday and Tuesday the headmaster let the boys have the preceding Saturday off as well, giving them a four-day exeat. For Törless, however, there wasn't enough time to make the long journey home; he had hoped his parents might visit, but his father had urgent business to attend to at the Ministry and his mother didn't feel up to making the exhausting trip alone.

It was only when he received their letter telling him, amid a host of affectionate consolations, that they wouldn't be able to come that he realized it suited him perfectly. At this point it would have been almost a disruption – or at least slightly awkward for him – if he had had to face his parents.

Many of the others had been invited to nearby estates. Dschjusch, whose parents owned a beautiful property a day's drive away, was going there, taking Beineberg, Reiting and Hofmeier with him. He had invited Basini as well, but Reiting had ordered him to decline. Törless made the excuse that he still didn't know whether his parents were coming or not; he was in no mood for the innocent and frivolous entertainment of a house party.

By midday on Saturday the vast school building was silent and virtually deserted.

When he walked along the corridors his footsteps echoed from one end to the other; as most of the masters had either gone hunting or on various other trips, there was no one to take an interest in him. The few other boys who had remained behind only saw each other at mealtimes, which were now served in a small room next to the empty refectory; afterwards their footsteps disappeared back into the great maze of rooms and corridors, as if the silence of the place had swallowed them, and for the rest of the time their existence was no more noticeable than the spiders and woodlice in the cellars and attics.

From Törless's class only he and Basini had stayed behind, apart from one or two who were in the sanatorium. Before Reiting left, Törless had had a private word with him about Basini. Reiting was worried that he would take advantage of the occasion to ask one of the masters to protect him, so he made Törless promise to keep a close eye on him.

But Törless didn't need a reason to concentrate his attention on Basini.

The hustle and bustle of carriages drawing up at the main entrance, servants carrying trunks, boys laughing and joking as they said goodbye to each other, had barely died away before he was seized by the overpowering awareness that he was alone with Basini.

After lunch, Basini was sitting in his usual place at the front of the classroom, writing a letter, while Törless sat in the far corner at the back and tried to read.

It was the same book as before, the first time he had opened it for a while, and he had planned the situation in detail: Basini in front, himself behind, with his eyes fixed on the other boy, boring into him. This was how he wanted to read. With every page he sank deeper and deeper into Basini. This was how it had to happen; it was how he would discover the truth without letting life, this living, breathing, complex and ambivalent life, slip through his fingers...

But it was no good – as always when he had planned something in too much detail. It lacked spontaneity, and his mood soon changed to the stubborn, cloying ennui that always seemed to cling to any of his overly self-conscious attempts.

Angrily he tossed the book onto the floor. Basini looked round, startled, but quickly went back to his letter.

The hours and minutes dragged on into dusk. Törless just sat there, bored out of his mind. The only thing that relieved the all-enveloping droning sensation was the sound of his watch ticking: it wagged away behind the listless hours like a little tail. Everything in the room was blurred, indistinct... Basini must have finished writing his letter long ago... "Ah," thought Törless, "he probably doesn't dare to light the lamp." Was he even still sitting in his place? Before he looked out of the window at the bleak, twilit countryside his eyes had to become accustomed to the darkness in the room. "Oh yes, that shadow over there, the one that isn't moving, that must be him. He sighed just now – once, or was it twice – or is he asleep?"

A servant came and lit the lamps. Basini gave a start, rubbed his eyes. Then he got up and fetched a book from his locker and seemed to be getting on with some work.

Törless was dying to speak to him, and so to stop himself he hurried out of the room.

That night he came close to throwing himself on Basini. After a day of mind-numbing boredom his sensual nature was violently aroused, but luckily he fell asleep just in time.

Another day went by. It brought only the same empty, unproductive calm. The silence, the ceaseless anticipation left him in a state of overexcitement, the constant effort of concentration took up all his mental energy to the point where he was unable even to think.

Shattered, and so disappointed with himself that he was wracked with self-doubt, he went to bed early.

For a while he lay there half-asleep, restless and burning, and then he heard Basini come in.

Without moving a muscle he watched the vague shape as it walked past the foot of his bed; he heard the sound of clothes being taken off; then the rustle of covers as they were pulled up over a body.

He held his breath, although by now he was in no state to hear anything. And yet he couldn't help feeling that Basini wasn't asleep either, that like him he was lying there in the darkness, alert and listening.

The quarter-hours turned into hours. Every now and then there was the faint sound of a body turning over in its sleep.

Törless was kept awake by a bizarre state of agitation. The day before it had been the sensual images created by his imagination that had brought on this fever. Only at the very end had they begun to have a connection with Basini, as if the unyielding hand of sleep that always chased them away had held back at the last minute, leaving him with just a vague memory. Tonight, however, he had felt a compulsive urge to go over to Basini's bed from the very start. As long as he sensed that Basini was awake and listening for him, then it was as much as he could do to control this desire; but now that the other boy was almost certainly asleep, this was joined by a savage impulse to jump on him like a wild animal attacking its prey.

Already he could feel his muscles twitching, ready to make him sit up and get out of bed. And yet he was unable to shake off his immobility.

"But what am I actually going to do to him?" he wondered, almost talking out loud in his anxiety. Because he had to admit that the cruelty and sensual desire in him didn't seem to be aimed at anything in particular. If he were to fling himself on Basini, he would be terribly embarrassed. So didn't he even want to give him a thrashing? Heaven forbid! How on earth would that help assuage his feelings of arousal? The thought of various boyish vices went through his mind, but instinctively he recoiled in disgust. Show himself up in front of someone else? Never!...

Yet the stronger his feelings of revulsion became, the more he felt impelled to go over to Basini's bed. Although he was well aware of the folly of such a course of action, in the end it was as if a physical impulse was dragging him out of bed like a rope. And so, as the images faded from his mind and he kept telling himself that the best thing to do would be to go to sleep, almost mechanically he sat up in bed. Slowly, very slowly – all the time realizing that this psychological restraint could only gain ground over his opponent step by step – he got up. First an arm... then his upper body, then he slipped one knee out from under the covers... and then... and then suddenly he was hurrying barefoot across the room and sitting on the edge of Basini's bed.

Basini was asleep.

He even seemed to be having a pleasant dream.

Törless still hadn't regained control of himself. For a moment he sat perfectly still, staring down at the sleeping face. Flashing through his mind were those brief, disjointed thoughts, the simple observations that come to us when we lose our balance, fall over, or when something is snatched from our hand. Then without knowing what he was doing he took Basini by the shoulder and shook him awake.

The sleeping boy stretched lazily a couple of times, then woke with a start and looked up at Törless with dream-filled eyes.

Törless was gripped with fear; he was totally at a loss: for the first time he realized exactly what he was doing, and had no idea what he ought to do next. He felt utterly ashamed. The pounding of his heart was audible. Explanations and excuses were on the tip of his tongue... He was going to ask Basini if he had any matches, if he knew what time it was...

Meanwhile Basini kept staring vacantly up at him.

Without saying a word, he had by now let go of Basini's shoulder; he had by now shifted to the end of the bed, ready to creep back to his own – but then Basini suddenly seemed to understand what was happening and sat up.

Törless stood at the foot of the bed, hesitating. Basini gave him another searching look, then quickly got up, put on his coat and slippers and shuffled across the room towards the door.

In a flash Törless knew this wasn't the first time.

On the way out he got the key to the attic room from under his pillow.

Basini led him straight there. Although they had always kept the room's existence a secret from him, he seemed to know the way perfectly. He held the crate steady as Törless jumped down onto it, moved the scenery aside carefully and quietly like a well-trained flunkey.

Törless opened the door and they went in. As he went to light the lamp he had his back to Basini.

When he turned round, Basini was standing in front of him completely naked.

Instinctively he stepped back. The unexpected sight of this snow-white body, behind which the red of the walls took on the aspect of blood, both dazzled and disconcerted him. Basini had a beautiful physique; still showing few traces of manhood, it had all the delicate slenderness of a chaste young girl. For Törless, this image of nudity was like hot white flames blazing through his nervous system. He was powerless to resist this beauty, its authority. Up till now he hadn't realized what beauty was. After all, what did he know of art! For someone his age, used to being out in the fresh air, old paintings were dull and incomprehensible.

But now it came to him by way of sensuality. A surprise attack. From the bare flesh radiated a beguiling warm breath, a soft, lascivious cajolery; and yet there was something compelling and solemn about it that made him want to join his hands in prayer.

Once the initial shock had passed he felt ashamed, as much of himself as for the other boy. "This is a man, after all!" The thought filled him with indignation, yet he sensed that if it had been a girl, things would have been little different.

Filled with embarrassment, he snapped at Basini: "What's got into you! You'd better... right now!..."

It was the other boy's turn to be disconcerted; hesitantly, not taking his eyes off Törless for a second, he bent down and picked up his coat.

"Sit over there!" Törless ordered. Basini did as he was told. Törless leant against the wall, hands behind his back.

"Why did you take your clothes off? What were you expecting?"

"I just thought…"

Basini hesitated.

"What were you thinking of?"

"The others…"

"What others?"

"Beineberg and Reiting…"

"What about Beineberg and Reiting? What did they do? You have to tell me everything! I demand it, do you hear? Even though I've already heard about it from them." Törless blushed at this clumsy attempt at lying. Basini bit his lip.

"Well?"

"No, please don't make me tell you! Please don't! I'll do anything you want, but don't make me tell you… Oh, you've got such a strange way of tormenting me!…" There was hatred, fear and desperate pleading in Basini's eyes. Unwittingly, Törless relented.

"I've no intention of tormenting you. I simply want to get you to admit the truth. It might even be for your own good."

"But I haven't done anything worth talking about."

"Oh really? So why did you get undressed just now?"

"Because they made me."

"Why did you do what they told you? Are you a coward? A miserable, pathetic coward?"

"I'm not a coward! Don't say that!"

"Hold your tongue! If you're afraid of them hitting you, just wait till I get started!"

"I'm not afraid of them hitting me."

"Oh no? So what are you afraid of?"

Törless began speaking calmly again. He was already annoyed with himself for making vicious threats. But they had slipped out unintentionally, because he had the impression that Basini was taking liberties with him that he wouldn't take with the others.

"So if, as you say, you're not afraid, then what is it?"

"They say that if I do whatever they want, then after a while everything will be forgiven."

"Who by? The two of them?"

"No, by all of you."

"How can they make promises like that? I'm entitled to have my say as well!"

"They say they'll take care of that!"

This came as a shock to Törless. He was reminded of what Beineberg had said, that if the occasion arose Reiting was quite capable of treating him in the same way he did Basini. And if it should come to a conspiracy against him, what could he do about it? He was no match for them in matters of that sort, and in any case how far would they go? As far as with Basini? His whole being rebelled against such a pernicious notion.

Several minutes went by. Törless knew he had neither the nerve nor the willpower for these Machiavellian intrigues, but only because they didn't interest him, because he never felt fully engaged with them; he always had more to lose than he stood to gain. Yet if things turned out differently he sensed that he possessed a quite different type of tenacity and daring. He just had to know when it was the right moment to stake everything on one roll of the dice.

"Did they tell you anything else... what they were thinking of doing... something that concerns me?"

"Anything else? No. They just said they would take care of things."

Nonetheless... there was still a danger... hidden away somewhere... lying in wait for him: every step he took might be a trap, every night could be the last before battle was joined. Along with this thought came terrible uncertainty. It was no longer a question of casually looking on, playing games with mysterious visions – this was reality, unvarnished and with all its nasty sharp edges.

They continued their earlier conversation.

"And so what do they do with you?"

Basini didn't reply.

"If you're serious about mending your ways then you have to tell me everything."

"They make me take my clothes off."

"Yes yes, I noticed… and then?…"

There was a slight pause, and then Basini suddenly said: "Various things."

He spoke in an effeminate, almost provocative voice.

"So you're their… miss… mistress?"

"Oh no, I'm their friend!"

"How can you have the nerve to say that?"

"It's what they say themselves."

"What?…"

"Yes, Reiting says it."

"Reiting?"

"Yes, he's very friendly with me actually. Usually I just have to take my clothes off and read to him from a history book; something about Ancient Rome and the Caesars, the Borgias or Tamerlane… you know the sort of stuff, all those bloodthirsty epics. At those times he's even quite affectionate with me.

"And then afterwards he usually beats me…"

"Afterwards?… Oh, right!"

"Yes. He says that if he didn't beat me then he would have to accept that I'm a man, and he wouldn't be allowed to be so gentle and affectionate with me. But this way I'm just a possession, so he doesn't need to feel awkward."

"What about Beineberg?"

"Oh, Beineberg is dreadful. Don't you think his breath smells?"

"Shut up! What I think or don't think is none of your business! Just tell me what Beineberg does with you!"

"Much the same as Reiting, except… but you mustn't insult me again…"

"Get on with it."

"Except… in a more roundabout way. He always begins by lecturing me about my soul. About how I've corrupted it, although only its outer vestibule so to speak. Compared with the inner sanctum this is insignificant, superficial. It just has to be mortified; that was how many great sinners became saints. So seen from a higher level the sin isn't terribly serious: you just have to take it to its most extreme point and it will destroy itself of its own accord. Then he makes me sit and stare into a piece of crystal…"

"He hypnotizes you?"

"No, he says that whatever is floating on the surface of my soul has to be put to sleep and rendered powerless. Only then can he make contact with my soul."

"How does he make contact with it?"

"It's an experiment that he's never managed to get to work. He sits down and makes me lie on the floor so he can rest his feet on my body. I have to be sleepy and relaxed from staring at the crystal. Then all of a sudden he tells me to bark. He describes to me exactly how to do it: softly, more of a whimper, like a dog barking in its sleep."

"What's the point of that?"

"How do I know? He gets me to grunt like a pig as well, and keeps telling me that there's something of a pig in me. But it's not meant as an insult; he says it very quietly, in a kind way, so that – to use his words – it's imprinted on my mind. According to him I might have been a pig in a previous existence, and it has to be drawn out of me to remove the danger."

"And do you believe all this?"

"Good God, no: I don't think he really believes it himself. In any case it's got nothing to do with that. And why would I believe in that sort of thing? Who believes in the soul nowadays – let alone transmigration? I know perfectly well that I did something wrong, but I was hoping that I could put it right. There's no need for hocus-pocus to do that. I'm not going to lose any sleep over how and why I did it. Things like that happen so quickly, almost of their own accord; it's only afterwards that you realize you've done something stupid. But if he gets pleasure from trying to find something supernatural in it, then it's all the same to me. But in the meantime I have to submit to his will. If only he would stop pricking me…"

"What?"

"Yes, with a needle – oh, not very hard, just to see how I react… or if it leaves a visible trace on my body. But it still hurts. According to him the doctors don't understand anything about it; I haven't paid much attention to how he says he can prove it, all I remember is that he talks a lot about fakirs, who, while they are contemplating their soul, are insensible to physical pain."

"Oh yes, I know about those theories. But you said this wasn't everything."

"No, definitely not: as I said, in my opinion it's just a diversion. Afterwards there are periods of fifteen minutes or so when he doesn't say a word and I've no idea what's going on inside his head. Then suddenly he flies into a rage like a thing possessed and demands that I do things – far worse than anything Reiting makes me do."

"And you do everything he tells you?"

"What choice have I got? I want to go back to being a respectable person and to be left in peace."

"And you think that what's happening in the meantime is neither here nor there?"

"But I can't do anything about that."

"Now, think carefully before you answer my questions: how did you come to steal?"

"How? I needed the money urgently, that's how. I'd run up debts at the restaurant in town and they weren't prepared to wait any longer. And I was sure that I'd be getting some money in the post any day. No one in the class would lend me a penny: some because they didn't have any themselves, and the misers because they're always delighted when the extravagant ones are short of funds at the end of the month. I certainly didn't want to deceive anyone: I just wanted to borrow it secretly..."

"That wasn't what I meant," interrupted Törless, who was losing patience with this recital that was clearly helping unburden Basini's conscience. "The question was: how and why could you do it, what did you feel? What was going on in your head at the time?"

"Nothing at all. It only took a second or two – I didn't feel anything, I didn't stop to think: it just happened."

"And the first time with Reiting? The first time he made you do these things? Do you understand me?..."

"It was really unpleasant. Because I was being forced to do it. Although... if you think about it there are plenty of people who do it because they want to, because they enjoy it, without anyone knowing. That can't be so terrible."

"But you did it because you were forced to. You degraded yourself. Like crawling through excrement just because someone told you to."

"That's true – but I had to do it."

"No you didn't."

"But they would have given me a thrashing, reported me; all the blame and disgrace would have come crashing down on me."

"Fair enough, but forget about that for a moment. Listen, I want you to tell me something else. You spent a lot of money with Božena. You bragged to her, puffed yourself up, flaunted your masculinity. So you want to be a man? You don't just want to talk about it, don't just want to… you know what I mean… you actually want to be a man, deep down inside? And then someone comes along and asks you to do degrading things and you're too much of a coward to refuse: doesn't that tear your whole being apart? Aren't you even vaguely frightened that something unspeakable has happened inside you?"

"For God's sake, I don't understand. I've no idea what you're talking about. I can't tell you any more than I have already."

"Look here: I'm going to order you to get undressed again."

Basini smiled.

"And to lie on the floor at my feet. Don't laugh! I'm actually ordering you, do you hear! If you don't do what you're told this instant then you'll soon find out what's in store for you when Reiting gets back!… Fine. So you see: now you're lying naked at my feet. You're even trembling – are you cold? Now I can spit on you whenever I like. Press your face hard onto the floorboards; doesn't the dust look strange? Like a landscape with clouds and rocks as big as houses? I could stick needles in you too. There are some over there in the alcove, by the lamp. Can you feel them in your flesh already?… But I don't want to… I could get you to bark, like Beineberg does, make you lick the dust from the floor like a pig, I could make you perform certain acts – you know what I'm talking about – and at the same time sigh: 'Oh, my dear Mother…'" Törless halted this blasphemy in mid-flow. "But I don't want to; I don't want to, do you hear me!"

Basini was crying. "You're tormenting me…"

"Yes, I'm tormenting you. But that's not my intention. I just want to know one thing: when I stick all this in you like knives, what does it feel like? What happens to you? Does something shatter inside you? Tell me! Like a glass that smashes into a thousand pieces although there's no sign of a crack in it? Hasn't the image that you had of yourself suddenly blown away on the breeze, while another one leaps out of the darkness and takes its place like a picture from a magic lantern? Do you really not understand what I'm saying? I can't make it any clearer; it's up to you to tell me!…"

Basini was still crying. His girlish shoulders were shaking, he just kept repeating the same thing over and over again: "I don't know what you want. I can't explain it any more than I have. It just happened in a flash, there was nothing I could do to stop it. You would have behaved exactly the same as I did."

Törless didn't reply. He stayed where he was, leaning against the wall, exhausted, not moving, staring straight ahead into the void.

"If you were in my position you would have behaved exactly the same" – that was what Basini had said. If that were so, then events were no more than a necessity, something you did calmly and quietly without making a fuss.

Törless's self-consciousness rebelled against the effrontery of this suggestion, reacted with contempt. And yet this revolt of his whole being didn't seem to offer adequate guarantees. "…Yes, I would have more strength of character than him, I wouldn't stand for any such effrontery – but is that the most important thing? Is it important that out of moral strength, decency, for honourable motives that at the moment are secondary to me, I would behave any differently? No, it's not important to know how I would behave, but to know that if one day I *did* behave like Basini, would I feel, like he does, that it was completely unremarkable? That's the main thing: that my knowledge of myself would be as simple and unclouded by doubts as his is…"

This thought, which came to him in disjointed, tangled fragments that were constantly being re-examined, added a faint yet intimate element of suffering to his contempt for Basini, one that was far more unsettling for his inner equanimity than any sense of morality, and which sprang from the memory of an emotion which he had recently felt and was unable to get out of his mind: that when he had found out from Basini that Reiting and Beineberg might be a threat to him he had been scared. Simply scared, like when you are attacked unexpectedly, and without thinking he had responded in a flash, looked for a way of retaliating as well as somewhere to take cover. He had done this in a moment of real danger, and the emotions he had experienced as a result, these rash, unthinking impulses, now began to tantalize him. He tried to unleash them again within himself, but to no avail. But he realized that they had deprived this threat of the possibility of being in any way unusual or ambiguous.

Nonetheless, it was the same threat that he had foreseen a few weeks earlier in the same place. The night when he had been so strangely frightened by this room, which after the warm, brightly lit classrooms was like a relic from the Middle Ages, and by Beineberg and Reiting, who from being fellow pupils suddenly seemed to become quite different, something sinister, bloodthirsty, characters from another world. At the time it had been a form of metamorphosis, a great leap for him, as if he had woken after sleeping for a hundred years and had seen his surroundings with completely different eyes.

And yet it was still the same threat… That was what he kept repeating to himself, while trying to compare the memory of these two feelings.

In the meantime Basini had got up from the floor; he noticed Törless's fixed, absent-minded gaze, quietly gathered up his clothes and crept out of the room.

Törless saw him as if through a mist, but let him go without saying anything. His attention was concentrated on trying to locate the precise point where this change in his inner perspective had taken place.

But whenever he approached it it moved away, as if he were trying to compare something very close with something far away; his memory never managed to seize hold of both feelings at once, and between them came another feeling, a kind of faint click which on a physical level was not unlike the barely perceptible muscular sensations that occur when the eye shifts in a new direction. Yet at the decisive moment it was always this that held his attention, the act of making a comparison took the place of the object that was being compared, there was a slight jolt and everything stopped.

And each time he started again from the beginning.

This almost mechanical process left him in something like an icy, waking dream, and for a while he just stood where he was, motionless.

Then he was woken by a thought that brushed against his senses like a warm, gentle hand. A thought that seemed so obvious that he was surprised it hadn't occurred to him a long time ago.

It was a thought that did little more than register the experience that it had just had. Anything that looks vast and mysterious from a distance always seems simple when viewed from close up, and takes on normal, everyday proportions. It is as if there is an invisible boundary around human beings. Everything that approaches us from beyond this borderline is like a mist-covered ocean full of gigantic, constantly changing shapes; anything that crosses this border, becomes an action, touches our lives, is small, clear and of natural, human dimensions. And between the life we lead and the one we feel, whose existence we can only guess at and which we only see from a distance, there is an invisible boundary, like a narrow gateway where the images of past events have to make themselves smaller before they can find their way inside us.

And yet however closely this resembled his own experience, he kept staring at the ground, lost in thought.

"What an extraordinary idea," he said to himself.

Eventually he got back to bed. He had virtually banished all thoughts from his mind; thinking was so difficult, it achieved so little. What he had discovered about his friends' clandestine activities probably passed through his subconscious, but it left him as indifferent and impassive as an article in a foreign newspaper.

There was nothing more to expect from Basini. Although that was his problem! But it was such an unknown quantity, and he was so tired, so utterly exhausted. Maybe it was just an illusion – no more than that.

All that remained was the image of Basini, his naked, radiant flesh, drifting like the scent of lilacs among the half-light of sensations and impressions that ushers in sleep. Even his moral outrage had disappeared. Finally he fell asleep.

No dreams came to disturb his rest. But a delicious warmth kept spreading soft rugs beneath his body, and it was this that eventually woke him. He almost cried out: Basini was sitting beside his bed! The next moment, with almost wild haste the other boy had pulled off his nightshirt, slipped under the covers and pressed his naked, trembling body against Törless.

Before he had recovered from the shock of this invasion, he pushed Basini away.

"What's got into you?…"

But Basini began to plead. "Oh, don't start that again! There's no one else like you. The others don't despise me the way you do; they just pretend so later on they can look even more different. But you? You're just you! You're younger than me, although you're stronger... we're both younger than the others... you're not rough and boastful like they are... you're so gentle... I love you!..."

"What? What do you mean? What do you want? Go away – get away from me!" Literally in pain, Törless pushed Basini's shoulder to make him move away. But he was fixated by the presence of this soft, unfamiliar flesh burning so close to his own, and which seemed to surround him, stifle him. And all the time Basini was whispering: "Yes... oh yes... please, I'm begging you... I'll gladly do anything you want."

Törless didn't know what to say. As Basini was speaking, as he wasted valuable seconds thinking, trying to make up his mind, it was as if the same dark-green ocean had washed over his senses again. Only Basini's frantically repeated words stood out, like the shimmering of tiny silverfish.

He kept pushing him away with both arms, but a damp, heavy warmth seemed to weigh them down; and then his muscles went limp, he forgot all about them... It was only when a new, glittering word appeared that he woke up, and all of a sudden – as if in a terrifying, incomprehensible reality, a kind of dreamworld – he felt his hands drawing Basini closer.

Desperately he tried to wake up, cry out to himself: "Basini is playing a trick on you: he's trying to drag you down to his level so you won't be able to despise him any more." But the words died in his throat; nowhere in the vast school building was there a single sound; in the corridors and passages the dark tides of silence lay motionless, as if sleeping.

He tried to regain his self-control; but like black-clad sentinels the silent tides were at every door.

So he abandoned the search for words. The sensual desire that had taken advantage of every moment of despair to worm its way into him gradually had now reached its peak. It was lying naked at his side, draped its soft black cloak over his head. It whispered sweet nothings of surrender in his ear, while its warm fingers thrust aside any lingering doubts and duties as being in vain. And it murmured: "When you are alone, nothing is forbidden."

Just as he was about to be swept away he came to himself for a few seconds, and clung desperately to a single thought: "It isn't me doing this!... It isn't me!... Tomorrow I'll be my usual self again!... Tomorrow..."

15

ON TUESDAY EVENING the first boys started arriving back at school. Others were travelling on the overnight sleeper train. The whole place was plunged into a constant uproar.

Törless greeted his classmates with sullen ill humour; he had forgotten nothing. Not only that, they brought with them a breath of fresh air, elegance and sophistication from the outside world. He was ashamed that he had grown to love the sultry atmosphere of the cramped rooms and dormitories.

In fact, he felt ashamed most of the time now. Not so much for allowing himself to be led astray – for in schools like this it was far from unusual – than for the fact that he couldn't help but feel a sort of affection for Basini, while at the same time being even more convinced that he was a despicable and degenerate individual.

He had frequent secret assignations with him. He took him to all the hiding places that Beineberg had shown him, although, as he wasn't well versed in such surreptitious escapades, Basini, who was more ingenious in that respect, soon took the lead.

At night, however, the pangs of jealousy that forced him to keep watch on Beineberg and Reiting prevented him from sleeping.

But the two of them seemed to be avoiding Basini. Perhaps he had already begun to bore them. Whatever the case, they appeared to have undergone something of a change. Beineberg had become grim and uncommunicative; when he did say anything it was only to make mysterious allusions to some imminent event. Reiting's interest had apparently moved on: with his usual skill he was busy spinning the web of some new intrigue with which he hoped to gain favours for himself, terrifying the others by artfully uncovering their little secrets.

Whenever the three of them were alone together, Beineberg and Reiting seemed to be determined that Basini would soon have to be made to come up to the little room or to the main attic again. Törless used every excuse he could think of to try to postpone this, yet he suffered constantly from this covert collusion with them.

Only a few weeks earlier he would have found such a state of affairs quite incomprehensible, because, if only as a result of his upbringing, he had always been a normal, strong, healthy boy.

It must not be assumed from this, however, that Basini aroused – even momentarily and confusedly – what could strictly speaking be called desire in Törless. While something not dissimilar to passion had certainly been awoken in him, to give it the name of love would be only an incidental and imprecise description, in the same way that Basini himself was no more than a temporary substitute for its true aim. Even when Törless debased himself with him it never satisfied his desire, which grew beyond Basini and became a new hunger that had no apparent purpose.

At first it was just the nakedness of the slender, boyish body that bedazzled him.

The impression it made was no different from what he would have experienced if he had been confronted with a young girl, her form still devoid of sexual attributes. It was overwhelming, astonishing. And it was the spontaneous purity of the moment that had given his relationship with Basini the appearance of an inclination – this wonderful new sensation of disquiet. All the other elements of desire played little part in it: they had already existed when he first started going to Božena, in fact long before then. It was the mysterious, aimlessly drifting and melancholy sensuality of budding youth, so like the damp, dark, fecund soil of spring, or those obscure subterranean streams that take the first opportunity to burst their banks.

The scene in which Törless had taken part was this very opportunity. A combination of surprise, misunderstanding, failure to appreciate the extent of the effect it had had on him, all conspired to break open the secluded hiding places in his soul where everything that was furtive, forbidden, sultry, uncertain and solitary had gathered, and to guide these obscure stirrings towards Basini. There they promptly came up against something warm, something that breathed, sweet-scented flesh, something that gave form to his ill-defined and shifting dreams and their particular beauty, instead of the corrosive ugliness with which Božena had infected them in her well of loneliness. It threw open the door of life to them, and in this gathering twilight everything mingled together, desires and reality, wild fantasies and impressions still warm from the touch of life, sensations that came to him from outside and flames that shot up to greet them from deep inside him, engulfing them until they were beyond recognition.

Yet for Törless these details were now indistinguishable: all he had was a hazy, incoherent feeling which in his initial surprise he quite understandably mistook for love.

But he quickly learnt to be more discerning. He was now buffeted by constant agitation. No sooner had he picked something up than he put it down again. He was unable to have a conversation with his classmates without lapsing into silence for no reason, or changing the subject a dozen times. There were even moments when he was overcome with shame in mid-sentence and would blush, begin to stammer and had to look away...

During the day he tried to avoid Basini. If he wasn't able to stop himself from looking at him, he was nearly always disappointed. Basini's every gesture filled him with disgust, the vague shadows of his illusions gave way to a cold, dull, pale light, and his soul shrivelled until there was nothing left except the memory of his original desire, which now seemed as incomprehensible as it was repugnant. It was as if he were trying to thrust his foot deep into the ground and huddle up to escape the clutches of this excruciating sense of shame.

He wondered what the other boys, his parents, the masters would say if they found out about his secret.

But it was with this last wound that his torments always came to an end. He would be seized with a cold feeling of lassitude; his hot, flaccid flesh would tauten with a shudder of contentment. At these moments he quietly let other people pass him by; yet there wasn't one of them for whom he didn't feel a certain disdain. He secretly suspected everyone he spoke to of the most appalling acts.

What was more, he thought they were all devoid of shame. He didn't believe they were capable of suffering in the way he did. Unlike him they didn't wear a crown of thorns woven by a guilty conscience.

He, however, had the impression that he had just woken from the pangs of death; he was like someone who has been brushed by the discreet and gentle hands of the Dark Angel; someone who can never forget the still, silent wisdom that is acquired from enduring a long illness

When he was in this frame of mind he felt happy, and there were times when he looked back and longed to experience it again.

It was then that he began to view Basini with indifference again, to laugh off the cheap and loathsome aspects of his character. He knew he was debasing himself, but this took on new meaning. The more sordid and degrading the things that Basini offered him became, the greater the contrast with the feeling of exquisite suffering that usually followed.

He would withdraw to some quiet corner from where he could observe unnoticed. When he closed his eyes he was filled with a kind of insistent yearning, but when he opened them again he was never able to find anything that could be compared with this sensation. And then *suddenly* he would think of Basini, and this thought kept growing until everything else was distorted, leaving him disorientated. It no longer seemed to bear any relationship to him, nor did it seem to be associated with Basini. Feelings and emotions would swish and swirl around him like lascivious women in high-necked dresses, their faces hidden by masks.

He couldn't put a name to any of these feelings, and had no idea what he might retain from them; but therein lay the exhilarating temptation. He no longer recognized himself, and it was precisely this that led his desires towards unbridled and shameless debauchery, like those wild carousals where the lights suddenly go out and no one is quite sure whom they are lying with on the floor and smothering with kisses.

In years to come, once he had outgrown the events of adolescence, Törless would become a young man of refined and delicate sensitivities. His was one of those aesthetic, intellectual natures that take comfort from complying with the law and – at least partly – public morality, as this relieves them of having to think about crude and vulgar matters that are far removed from the subtle atmosphere of their inner lives, and yet along with this faintly ironic correctness show bored indifference for such matters whenever they are asked to express an interest in them. For the only thing that truly absorbs their interest is the development of the soul, the spirit or whatever we wish to call that element within us which we might glimpse between the lines of a book or the sealed lips of a portrait; which is sometimes woken in us when a solitary and persistent melody drifts away from us – crying out in the distance – strangely tugging at us with the slim, red thread of our blood. But this vanishes whenever we fill in an official form, build a machine, go to the circus or take part in countless other similar activities.

People of this kind are indifferent to things that only appeal to their sense of moral rectitude. So it follows that, later in life, Törless would never regret the things he did at this time. His needs were focused so single-mindedly on aesthetic matters that if someone were to tell him a not dissimilar story about the behaviour of a particular debauched individual it would never have entered his mind to express outrage. He would have despised this person, not for his debauchery, but for failing to better himself, so to speak; not for his excesses, but for the state of mind that led him to behave like that in the first place; for his stupidity, or because his mind lacked a sense of balance... in short, because he presented such a sad, inadequate and feeble spectacle. And he would have despised him equally had his vices been sexual dissipation or if he were a compulsive smoker or drinker.

Like all those who concentrate exclusively on heightening their intellectual capacities, the existence of sensual and disorderly emotions were of little importance to him. He liked to believe that a sense of enjoyment, artistic talent and a fastidious spiritual life were ornaments with which one could easily injure oneself. He considered it inevitable that someone with a rich and responsive inner life would always have things that he preferred other people not to know about, memories that he kept in secret compartments. All he asked was that one should know how to make subtle, discerning use of them later.

Thus it was that, when someone whom he had told about this youthful episode once asked him if he weren't sometimes still ashamed of it, he just smiled and gave this reply: "I certainly wouldn't deny that it was degrading. And why not? It's in the past now. But part of it will stay with me for ever: it's the small dose of poison that is necessary to prevent the soul from becoming too comfortably and too securely healthy, to make it sharper, more subtle and understanding.

"In any case, do you want to keep a record of the degradations that every great passion has seared into your soul? What of the times when lovers humiliate themselves intentionally! Those times of rapture when they lean over a deep well, or take it in turns to listen to each other's heart to see if they can hear the restless cats scratching at the walls of their dungeon? Just to feel themselves shudder! Just to be frightened by their own solitude at the edge of these dark, infamous depths! Just to seek refuge in each other against their fear of being alone!

"You only have to look young couples in the eye. What do you imagine they are saying? 'Think what you like, but you have no idea of the depths to which we are capable of sinking!' Those sparkling eyes which secretly mock anyone who can fail to know so many things, and the tender, loving pride of people who have been through hell together.

"And, like those lovers, I have been through all that – but on my own."

If Törless would express such opinions later in life, at this precise moment, however, when he found himself alone in a storm of desires and emotions, he was far from confident that the episode would have a happy ending. The enigmas that had recently tormented him were still having a vague effect, which rang out like a distant bass note behind everything he experienced. But he preferred not to think about it.

But there were times when he had to. At these moments he sunk into the depths of despair, and at the very memory of these things he was filled with a quite different and debilitating form of shame, in which the future seemed to hold out no hope for him.

And yet he was unable to account for any of this.

It was caused by the particular circumstances of life at the school. In a place where the tide of youthful energy was contained within the tall grey walls, all manner of voluptuous images piled up at random in the imagination, causing many a boy to go astray.

A degree of promiscuity was deemed manly, a sign of daring, the bold conquest of forbidden pleasures – especially when compared with most of the masters, who from their appearance were wasting away with respectability. As a result, any incitement to virtue was immediately – and absurdly – connected with anyone with sloping shoulders, a pot belly and spindly legs, and whose eyes, behind their glasses, were like those of lambs grazing innocently, as if life were a meadow full of the flowers of solemn edification.

In a word, the pupils at the school still knew nothing of life, and had not the slightest idea about the subtle distinctions that separate vulgarity from lechery and perversion from the absurd, which are among the first things that fill adults with revulsion when they hear about such behaviour.

Yet all these inhibiting elements, whose effectiveness cannot be overestimated, were something that Törless didn't possess. He had blundered into this misconduct out of pure naivety.

At the time he also still lacked the powers of moral resistance, the highly developed intellectual sensibility that he would later value so highly. And yet it was already dormant within him. Törless was adrift, all he saw were the shadows cast across his consciousness by something within him that he didn't recognize, and which he mistook for reality: yet he realized he had work to do on himself, on his soul, although he wasn't yet mature enough to do so.

All he knew was that he had followed something vague and indistinct along a path that led into the depths of his being – and this had left him exhausted. He had hoped to make extraordinary discoveries, but only succeeded in straying into the narrow, winding back roads of sensuality. Not out of perversion, but by going down a spiritual dead end.

It was this betrayal of a solemn ideal that gave him a vague sense of guilt; he was permanently dogged by secret disgust, an ill-defined anxiety, like someone walking in the dark and who doesn't know whether he is still on the path or if he has lost his way.

He did his best to stop thinking altogether. He simply got on with life, numb, vacant, saying little, putting all earlier questions out of his mind. The subtle delight that he had taken in degrading himself began to wane.

The feeling never quite left him; although when this brief period came to an end, and more decisions were taken about what should be done with Basini, he made no attempt to object.

16

THESE DECISIONS WERE TAKEN a few days later, when the three friends were alone together in the room in the attic. Beineberg looked very serious.

It was Reiting who spoke first: "Beineberg and I have come to the conclusion that the methods we've used on Basini so far aren't working. He's got used to the fact that he owes us obedience, it doesn't make him suffer any more; he's taken on that insolent familiarity that you find in servants. So I think it's time to go a step further. Do you agree?"

"It depends on what you're thinking of doing."

"It's not quite as simple as that. Obviously we should keep humiliating and crushing him. I'd like to see how far we can go with that. But how exactly we do it, well that's another matter entirely. Mind you, I've got one or two good ideas. For example, we could make him sing psalms of thanksgiving while we beat him – that would be quite fun: listening to someone singing where every note makes your flesh creep, if you see what I mean. Or we could make him go and find the most unsavoury objects and bring them to us. We could take him to Božena, make him read out his mother's letters, and then let her have whatever fun she likes. But there's no hurry to decide. We've got time to think about it, refine our ideas and come up with new ones. It might sound boring at the moment, but that's because we haven't worked out the details. Maybe we could hand him over to the whole class. That would be the wisest thing. In a large group, each person would only have to play a small part and he'd be torn to pieces. Besides, I enjoy seeing crowds in action: no one does anything in particular, and yet the tide gets higher and higher until everyone is engulfed. You'll see: no one will lift a finger, but there'll be a whirlwind. I can think of no greater pleasure than staging something like that."

"So what do you want to do first?"

"As I said, I'd prefer to save all that for later. In the meantime I'll be quite happy if we can get to the point – either by threatening or beating him – where he starts saying 'yes' to everything again."

"Everything?" said Törless, almost unintentionally. The two of them were staring each other in the eye.

"Come off it, don't play the innocent with me. After the last time you know perfectly well what I'm talking about…" Törless didn't reply. Had Reiting discovered something… or was he just testing the lie of the land? "…and I know that Beineberg told you what Basini gets up to."

Törless breathed a sigh of relief.

"Oh please, don't look so surprised. You did that before, and it wasn't all that terrible. In any case, Beineberg has already told me that he does the same thing with Basini." And with this, Reiting pulled a sarcastic face at Beineberg. Dealing someone a low punch quite openly and in front of other people was very much his style.

Beineberg didn't respond; he just sat where he was, lost in thought, and barely even opened his eyes.

"What's the matter, has the cat got your tongue? He's got this completely mad idea for Basini and wants to put it into operation before we do anything else. It's actually quite amusing."

Beineberg was still looking serious. He gave Törless a meaningful glance and then said: "Do you remember what we talked about that day behind the coat rack?"

"Yes."

"I've never mentioned it again, but that's because words alone serve no purpose. But believe me, I've often thought about it. And what Reiting just told you is true: I've done the same with Basini as he has. Perhaps I've gone a bit further. Because as I said when we had that conversation, I've always believed that sensuality might be the right path to take. So it was an experiment. It was where my research seemed to lead. But working haphazardly doesn't make sense. So I've spent whole nights thinking about how to go about it in a more systematic way.

"And now I think I've found one, so we're going to put it to the test. And then you'll see just how wrong you were. Everything that is said about the world is far from clear, things happen differently from how we imagine them. Yet we only discover this by approaching it from the reverse side, so to speak, by looking for those points where this perfectly natural explanation trips itself up; and now I think I can demonstrate the positive aspect – the other side of the coin!"

Reiting, who was pouring the tea, gave Törless a nudge. "Just listen to this!" he said, with a look of glee on his face. "It's really spiffing what he's come up with."

Beineberg quickly put out the lamp. In the darkness the flame under the little spirit burner threw a trembling bluish light across their faces.

"I've put the lamp out, Törless, because it's more suited to what we're talking about. If you're too stupid to understand these more profound questions, Reiting, you might as well go to sleep."

Highly amused, Reiting roared with laughter.

"So you remember our conversation. You yourself had just discovered a slight anomaly in mathematics – an example that shows that our thought process isn't always based on solid foundations, that there are gaps to leap across. It closes its eyes, stops and listens for a moment, yet it manages to land safely on the other side. We must have been in this state of despair for a long time, because in many areas our knowledge is full of gaping chasms, leaving nothing but fragments above a bottomless ocean.

"And yet we don't despair; in fact we have the impression that we're standing on solid ground. If we didn't have this unambiguous sense of security then we would commit suicide in desperation at the poverty of our intellect. This feeling goes with us everywhere, gives us cohesion, safeguards our reason like a mother holding her child in her arms. Once we understand this we can no longer deny the existence of the soul. As soon as we analyse our intellectual life and realize how inadequate our intelligence is, then we feel it quite literally. If this feeling didn't exist – do you see what I'm saying? – then we would just collapse like empty sacks.

"We have forgotten how to pay attention to this feeling, yet it's one of the most ancient feelings in the world. Thousands of years ago, people who lived thousands of miles from each other were already aware of it. As soon as we show an interest in things of this kind we can no longer deny that they exist. But I won't try to convince you with long speeches; I'll just give you enough detail so you can understand what's happening. The facts will provide all the proof you need.

"So if we accept that the soul exists, then it follows naturally that we can have no more burning desire than to re-establish contact with it, to become intimate with it again, to learn how best to use its energies and gain control of part of the supernatural powers that lie dormant deep inside them.

"Because all of this is possible, it's been achieved more than once – the miracles, the lives of the saints, the Indian seers all bear witness to such happenings."

"Just a minute," said Törless, interrupting him. "I think it's yourself that you're trying to convince with these beliefs. That must be why you had to put out the lamp. Would you speak like this if we were sitting with all the others while they were doing their geography or history prep, or writing letters home in a brightly lit classroom where one of the prefects might be strolling up and down between the desks? Hasn't it occurred to you that what you're saying might be rather outlandish, even slightly pretentious, as if we were a different species from them and came from another world that existed eight hundred years ago?"

"No, my dear Törless, I would say exactly the same thing. And besides, forever looking over your shoulder to see what other people are doing has always been one of your faults: you're not nearly independent enough. Writing letters home!

We're discussing matters of this kind and you're thinking about your parents! Who says they're capable of following us along this road? We're a whole generation younger, there might be experiences reserved for us that they have never dreamt of. At least that's my feeling. But what will all this talk achieve? I'm going to give you proof."

After a pause during which no one spoke, Törless said: "So how exactly do you intend to take possession of your soul?"

"I don't want to go into detail about that at the moment; and in any case, Basini has to be here for me to do it."

"You could at least give us a vague idea."

"If you like. History teaches us that there is only one way to do this: by descending deep within oneself. But that is precisely where the difficulty lies. In the past for example, when the soul still manifested itself through miracles, the saints could only achieve this by way of fervent inner prayer. At the time the soul must have been constituted differently, because nowadays that method always fails. Nowadays we have no idea what to do: the soul has changed, and unfortunately a long period of time has gone by during which no one has paid attention to this question, with the result that the connection has been irretrievably lost. Only after the most careful consideration will we be able to find another way. This has been on my mind constantly over the last few weeks. Hypnosis might prove to be the most successful means. But it's never been tried. People are satisfied with banal sleights of hand, which is why no one has experimented with other methods that might lead us to loftier heights. I'm not going to say any more now, except that I'm not intending to hypnotize Basini using the popular method, but my own, which I believe is similar to one used during the Middle Ages."

"Isn't he just too much, this Beineberg," laughed Reiting. "If only he had lived at the time when people were predicting the end of the world! He would have seriously believed that it was only because of this soul mumbo-jumbo of his that the human race still existed."

While Reiting mocked, Törless glanced at Beineberg. He noticed that his face had stiffened into a rigid mask, as if in intense concentration. The next moment he felt as if he were being seized by an ice-cold hand. The violence of his reaction frightened him; and then the fingers relaxed their grip. "Oh, it was nothing," said Beineberg. "Just an idea. I thought I had had an inspiration, a sign that seemed to be telling me what to do next..."

"From where I'm sitting you seem pretty exhausted," said Reiting jokingly. "I've always taken you for a tough fellow who only did this sort of thing for sport, but all of a sudden you look like a woman."

"Be quiet! You haven't the faintest idea what it's like to know that you're getting close to resolving questions of this kind, that every day you're on the point of having them in your grasp!"

"Let's not quarrel," said Törless – over the past few weeks he had become even more assertive – "as far as I'm concerned you can both do whatever you like; I don't believe in anything. Not in your sophisticated methods of torture, Reiting, nor in Beineberg's hopeful beliefs. I don't know what else to say. I'll just wait and see what you come up with."

"So when shall we do it?"

They decided it should be the following night.

17

TÖRLESS JUST LET IT GO AHEAD without offering any resistance. In any case, with these new developments he found that his feelings for Basini had very much cooled. It even turned out to be a lucky escape, by releasing him from a situation in which he vacillated between shame and desire without having the strength to break free. His disgust for Basini could now at least be clear and unambiguous, as if there were a risk that he himself might be defiled by the humiliations they were planning for him.

Apart from this his mind was elsewhere; he wasn't really capable of thinking, least of all about what had been preoccupying him.

It was only when he started climbing the stairs to the attic with Reiting – Beineberg had gone ahead with Basini – that the memory of what had happened to him became more vivid. The confident words that he had flung in Beineberg's face began to haunt him, and he longed to regain the resolve that he had shown then. His foot hesitated over every step. Yet his self-assurance refused to return. He could remember the thoughts he had had at the time, but they seemed to have left him far behind, as if they were just shadows of their former selves.

But eventually, as he was unable to find anything within himself, his curiosity focused on what was about to happen, and it was this that propelled him up the stairs.

Soon he was hurrying up the last few steps behind Reiting.

As the iron door creaked shut behind them, he told himself with a sigh that even if Beineberg's scheme turned out to be nothing more than a ludicrous conjuring trick it was at least founded on something solid and well-thought-out, whereas he was just a mass of confusion.

They sat on one of the crossbeams and waited in excited suspense as if they were at the theatre.

Beineberg and Basini were already there.

The conditions seemed ideal for his venture. The darkness, the stale air, the sweet, sickly smell that rose from the water butts created an atmosphere of drowsiness, of not being able to keep your eyes open, of weary, lethargic indifference.

Beineberg told Basini to get undressed. In the shadows his naked body took on a bluish, almost putrescent glow, and ceased to be in any way arousing.

Then suddenly Beineberg took the revolver from his pocket and pointed it at Basini.

This even made Reiting lean forward, ready to intervene if necessary.

But Beineberg just smiled. It was a peculiarly contorted expression, as if he didn't want to smile but the force of the fanatical words he was about to use had twisted his mouth out of shape.

As if paralysed, Basini fell to his knees and stared at the gun, his eyes bulging with fright.

"Get up," said Beineberg. "If you do exactly what I say then you won't get hurt – but if you oppose me in any way I'll just shoot you. Remember that!

"In a sense I am going to kill you, but you'll come back to life. Dying isn't as alien to our nature as you might think; we die every day – in deep, dreamless sleep."

And the same wild smile distorted his lips again.

"Go and kneel up there," he said, pointing to a broad horizontal beam that was at about waist height. "Like that, completely upright, keep yourself straight – you have to arch your back. Now look directly at this, but without blinking: you must open your eyes as wide as possible!"

Beineberg placed a small spirit lamp in front of and a little higher than Basini, so that he had to tip his head back slightly to look at it.

Although barely perceptible, after a while Basini's body seemed to begin swinging back and forth like a pendulum. The blue-tinted reflections moved up and down his skin. Every now and then Törless thought he could see his face contorting into an expression of fear.

After a while Beineberg asked: "Are you feeling sleepy?" This was the traditional question asked by hypnotists.

Then in a quiet, slightly hoarse voice he went on:

"Dying is simply a consequence of the way we live our life. We live from thought to thought, from feeling to feeling. Because our thoughts and feelings don't flow calmly and quietly like a stream, they 'fall into us' like a stone dropping down a well. If you study yourself closely you will see that your soul isn't something that changes colour in a series of gradual transitions, but that thoughts and ideas leap out of it like numbers out of a black hole. One minute you have a thought or feeling, the next another one appears as if from nowhere. If you pay attention, in the fleeting moment between two thoughts you can sometimes sense the utter darkness that exists there. Once we have grasped this, for us this moment is virtually the same as death.

"Our life consists of little more than setting out milestones and hopping from one to the other, thus experiencing many thousands of death moments every day. In a sense we only really live in the resting places that lie between them. That's why we have such a ridiculous fear of our final death, because after that there are no more milestones, and we tumble into the vast, unending abyss. For that way of life, this is utter negation. But it's only those who have never learnt to live any other way except from moment to moment who see it from that perspective.

"I call this the hopping malady, and the secret lies in overcoming it. We must learn to experience life as a gentle slide into awakening. The moment we succeed we are as close to death as we are to life. In worldly terms we are no longer alive, and yet we can no longer die, because as well as life we have also banished death. This is the moment of immortality, the moment when our soul leaves the narrow confines of our mind and enters the miraculous gardens of life.

"Now do exactly what I tell you.

"Let your mind go to sleep, keep your eyes fixed on this little flame... don't let your mind wander... focus your attention inwardly... keep your eyes on the flame... your thoughts are like a machine that is running slower... and slower... and slower... Keep looking inwards... until you reach the point where you can feel yourself but not your thoughts or emotions...

"I'll take your silence as a response. Keep your gaze turned inwards!..."

Several minutes went by.

"Can you feel the point?..."

No reply.

"Listen to me Basini: have you succeeded?"

Silence.

Beineberg stood up, and his gaunt shadow fell on the floor beside the beam. Above them, Basini could be seen swaying back and forth as if intoxicated with darkness.

"Turn sideways," Beineberg told him. "It's only the brain that is obeying me now," he muttered. "For a while it just works mechanically, until the last traces of the soul have disappeared from it. The soul is already somewhere else – in its next existence. It's no longer weighed down by the shackles of nature and its laws..." – and he turned to Törless – "it's no longer condemned to give weight and substance to a body. Lean forward Basini... yes, that's it... gradually... just move your body forward slightly... As soon as the final traces have been erased from the mind, then the muscles will relax and the empty body will collapse. Or it might continue to float, I'm not quite sure; the soul has left the body of its own accord, this isn't the usual type of death; perhaps the body will float in mid-air, because nothing, not the power of life or death will take responsibility for it any more... Lean forward slightly... a little farther."

All of a sudden the terrified Basini, who had been doing exactly as he was told, fell off the beam and crashed to the floor at Beineberg's feet.

Basini screamed in pain. Reiting roared with laughter. But when Beineberg, who had stepped back, realized that he had failed he let out a shriek of rage. In a flash he took off his leather belt, grabbed Basini by the hair and began to thrash him viciously. The terrible pressure that he had been under was released by his furious blows. Basini howled like a whipped dog, until every corner of the attic trembled with the sound.

During the whole scene Törless remained completely calm. He had secretly been hoping that something might happen to transport him back to the lost realm of his feelings. He had been aware all along that this was a foolish hope, and yet he had clung to it nonetheless. But it now seemed as if everything was over. The episode disgusted him. It was an unthinking disgust, inert and unspeaking.

Without saying a word he quietly got up and left. Completely mechanically.

Beineberg carried on thrashing Basini as if he would only stop once he was exhausted.

18

As HE LAY IN BED later that night, Törless had a sense of finality, that something had come to an end.

During the next few days he just got on quietly with his work; he didn't worry about anything. Reiting and Beineberg could continue putting their plan into action stage by stage, but he wanted nothing more to do with it.

Four days after the events in the attic, he was on his own, when Basini came up to him. He was a picture of misery, his face was pale and drawn, while in his eyes there was a constant, feverish flicker of anxiety. Casting frightened glances over his shoulder he blurted out: "You've got to help me! You're the only one who can! I can't stand it much longer, the way they're torturing me. I've put up with everything so far... but in the end they'll kill me!"

Törless would have preferred not to be involved in this conversation. After a moment he replied: "I can't help you. You're to blame for everything that's happening to you."

"But not long ago you were really nice to me."

"No I wasn't."

"But—"

"Don't even mention that. It wasn't really me... It was a dream... a passing whim... In fact I'm glad this latest depravity of yours has driven a wedge between us. It's the best thing that could have happened to me..."

Basini hung his head. He felt as if a dismal grey ocean of disillusionment lay between him and Törless... Törless was cold now, a totally different person.

Then suddenly he fell to his knees in front of him and pounded his head on the ground: "Help me! Help me! For God's sake help me!"

For a moment Törless hesitated. He had no desire to help Basini, but he wasn't sufficiently outraged to reject him. So he did what his first instinct told him: "Come to the attic tonight and I'll talk to you about it one last time." But he immediately regretted his words.

"Why go over all that again?" he thought. And then, as if he had given it some consideration, he added: "Actually it's no good: they'll see you."

"No they won't. They spent all last night with me, until first thing this morning; tonight they'll be fast asleep."

"All right then. But don't expect me to help you."

* * *

Törless had agreed to meet Basini against his own inner convictions. And these told him that everything was over, that there was nothing more to be gained. It was only a form of fastidiousness on his part, a stubborn conscientiousness that was nonetheless resigned to failure from the outset, which had whispered in his ear that he should go back over this ground one more time.

He wanted to get it over with as quickly as possible.

Basini had no idea how he should behave. He was so battered and bruised that he hardly dared move. Any personality that he had had seemed to have disappeared; only in his eyes was there a final trace, which seemed to cling to Törless, anxiously pleading with him.

So he waited to see what he was going to do.

It was Törless who eventually broke the silence. He spoke quickly, in a bored voice, as if it were a matter that had been dealt with a long time ago but which had to be looked at again purely for the sake of formality.

"I'm not going to help you. It's true that for a while I took an interest in you, but that's all in the past. The fact is you're nothing but a base, cowardly individual. That's all there is to it. So why should I stand up for you? Until recently I thought I could find other words, another way of describing you – but there is no other description except that you're a base coward. It might sound simplistic and meaningless, but that's really all there is to say. Ever since you got me involved with your unsavoury desires I've forgotten whatever else it was that I was originally looking for in you. I wanted to find a point a long way away from you, from where I could observe you... that was what interested me about you – and it was you who destroyed that... but I've gone far enough: I don't owe you any explanations. There's only one more thing: what do you feel now?"

"What am I supposed to feel? I just can't stand it any more."

"That they're doing terrible things to you and that you're in a lot of pain?"

"Yes."

"But is it only pain? You can feel that you're suffering, and you want to escape from it? Simply that? Nothing more complex?"

Basini didn't know how to reply.

"I see: my question obviously wasn't clear enough. But that isn't important. I want nothing more to do with you; I've already told you that. Your existence leaves me completely cold. You can do whatever you like…"

Törless was about to leave when Basini suddenly tore off his clothes and threw his arms round him. His body was covered in weals; it was repulsive, and the gesture was like that of an inept young prostitute. Törless turned away in disgust.

He had hardly gone more than a few steps into the darkness when he bumped into Reiting.

"What's this! So you're having secret assignations with Basini now, are you?"

Törless followed Reiting's gaze and looked back at Basini. Moonlight was shining through a skylight onto the very spot where he was standing. In the bluish glow his skin, with all its scars and bruises, looked like a leper's. Without thinking, he tried to explain.

"He was the one who came begging to me."

"What does he want?"

"For me to protect him."

"Well he chose the right person, didn't he?"

"I might have done it if this whole business hadn't become so boring."

Reiting didn't seem too pleased by this; angrily he turned to Basini.

"We'll teach you to plot behind our backs! Your guardian angel Törless will be there to witness it, and I'm sure he'll enjoy himself."

Törless had already started to walk away, but this pointed remark, which was clearly aimed at him, made him stop and turn round before he had time to think.

"No I won't, Reiting. I don't want anything more to do with this: it disgusts me."

"What, all of a sudden?"

"Yes, all of a sudden. At first I thought I could see something behind all this…" He wondered why he couldn't get this idea out of his mind…

"Ah, second sight!"

"Exactly. But now all I see is that you and Beineberg are a pair of crude, vulgar brutes."

"Oh, but you can't not watch Basini eating excrement," said Reiting sarcastically.

"I'm not interested any more."

"You were before!…"

"I've already told you: it was only because at the time Basini was a mystery to me."

"And now?"

"I don't see things as a mystery any more. They just happen: that's the only wisdom there is." He was surprised that the vocabulary that belonged to the lost realm of his emotions should suddenly come back to him like this. When Reiting retorted mockingly that "you don't need to look very far to find wisdom like that", he was suddenly filled with an angry sense of his own superiority, which drove him to use harsh words. For a second or two he despised Reiting so much that he would have gladly stamped him into the dirt.

"Mock as much as you like! But what *you're* doing is nothing but mindless, dismal, nauseating cruelty!"

Reiting shot a glance at Basini, who was listening closely.

"Watch what you're saying, Törless!"

"Nauseating, sordid – you heard me!"

It was Reiting's turn to lose his temper.

"I forbid you to insult us in front of Basini!"

"Ha! You're in no position to forbid me to do anything! Those days are over. I used to respect you and Beineberg, but now I see you for what you are: repulsive, brainless morons, no better than wild animals!"

"Shut your mouth or…"

Reiting seemed to be about to attack him. But Törless stepped back and shouted: "Do you think I'm going fight you? Basini isn't worth the effort. Do what you like to him, but just get out of my way!"

Reiting seemed to have had second thoughts about resorting to violence, and stepped aside. He didn't even lay a finger on Basini. But Törless knew what he was like, and realized that from now on he would have to watch his back against a constant, insidious threat.

19

TWO DAYS LATER, in the afternoon, Reiting and Beineberg came up to Törless.

He saw the malevolent look in their eyes. Beineberg now obviously blamed him for the ridiculous failure of his prophesies, and Reiting must have been fanning the flames.

"I hear you insulted us. And in front of Basini, to make matters worse. What gives you the right?"

Törless didn't answer.

"You know we won't stand for that sort of thing. But seeing as it's you and we're used to your moods and don't take much notice of them, we'll let sleeping dogs lie – as long as you do one thing."

Despite his friendly tone there was malice hovering some-where in Beineberg's eyes.

"Basini is coming to the room in the attic tonight; we're going to give him a thrashing for encouraging you to turn against us. When you see us leave the dormitory, you must follow."

Törless refused. "You can do whatever you like, but leave me out of it."

"We're going to have fun with Basini one last time, and then tomorrow we'll hand him over to the class, because he's start-ing to get disobedient."

"Do what you like."

"But you'll be there."

"No I won't."

"Basini has to be made to understand, with you as witness, that he's powerless against us. Last night he refused to do what we told him; we thrashed him half to death, but he still wouldn't submit. We have to go back to attacking him men-tally, humiliate him in front of you and then the whole class."

"But I'm not going to be there!"

"Why not?"

"Because."

Beineberg gave a deep sigh; then he came and stood right in front of Törless, as if he were about to spit venom in his face.

"Do you really think we don't know why? Do you think we don't know exactly what you got up to with Basini?"

"No more than you."

"Oh really. So I wonder why it was you that he chose as his patron saint? Well? Why it was that he put his trust in you? Do you take us for fools?"

Törless lost his temper: "I don't care what you know or don't know: just stop trying to drag me into this sordid business of yours!"

"So you're going to be offensive again!"

"You disgust me! This base behaviour of yours is utterly mindless! That's what I find so repulsive about you!"

"Listen: you have more than a few reasons to be grateful to us. If you think you're above us all of a sudden, when we've always been your masters, then you're making a big mistake. So are you coming tonight or not?"

"No!"

"My dear Törless, if you rebel and don't come, then you'll meet the same fate as Basini. You know perfectly well the circumstances in which Reiting found you. That will be enough. Whether we did more or less than you won't be of much help to you. We'll turn everything round so it points to you. You're far too weak-willed and not nearly clever enough when it comes to things like this to be able to protect yourself. So if you don't change your mind pretty rapidly we'll tell the rest of the class that you're Basini's accomplice. And then we'll see if he protects you. Is that understood?"

This stream of threats, issued first by Beineberg, then by Reiting, then by both of them together, passed over Törless's head like a thunderstorm. Once they had gone he rubbed his eyes as if he had been dreaming. But he knew Reiting: when he was in a rage he was capable of the vilest behaviour, and Törless's insults and insubordination seemed to have deeply offended him. And Beineberg? He had looked as if he were trembling with a hatred that had been building up inside him for years... and yet it was simply anger, because he had been made to look a fool in front of Törless.

Yet the more dramatic the events that were gathering above his head became, the more trivial and impersonal they seemed. Yes, the threats frightened him – but no more than that. The danger had just drawn him back into the whirlpool of reality.

He got into bed. He saw Beineberg and Reiting leave the dormitory with Basini, who was dragging his feet wearily as usual. But he didn't follow them.

Nonetheless he was still beset by terrible images. For the first time he thought of his parents with a little warmth. He sensed that he needed this quiet, safe territory for all the things that had been troubling him to evolve, to become more settled in his mind.

But what exactly was this? He didn't have time to give it any thought, or brood over what had happened. All he had was a burning desire to free himself from this confusing and tangled situation, a desire for silence, books. As if his soul were black soil beneath which the first seeds were beginning to shoot, although it wasn't possible to tell what they might eventually grow into. And he pictured a gardener watering his flower beds every day with steady, solicitous patience. He couldn't get this image out of his mind; its patient certainty seemed to have become the focus of all his longings. That was the only way! The only way, he thought. And his doubts and anxieties were thrust aside by the conviction that he should do his utmost to achieve this spiritual state.

The only thing that wasn't clear was what he ought to do first. Because the desire to reflect calmly on his situation only served to increase his loathing for the intrigues that he knew lay ahead. Not only that, he was genuinely afraid of the threats that had been directed at him. If the other two really tried to blacken his name in front of the class, the effort of defending himself would demand such a vast investment of energy that he could feel its ill effects even now. The mere thought of this turmoil, this meaningless struggle against an unfamiliar will and its bizarre intentions, sent a shudder of revulsion through him.

And then he suddenly remembered a letter he had received from his parents some time ago. It had been a reply to one he had written to them, in which he had tried, as best he could, to explain the peculiar feelings and emotions he was experiencing, although this was before the phase of sensual desire had begun. It was another thoroughly artless response, full of worthy and unimaginative moral advice, advising him to encourage Basini to go to the school authorities and admit his crime, so he could bring this degrading and dangerous state of subservience to an end.

He had read the letter again later, this time with Basini lying naked beside him on the thickly carpeted floor of the attic room. He had taken particular pleasure in letting the ponderous, facile, rational words dissolve on his tongue, while reflecting that his parents' overly clear and sunlit existence blinded them to the darkness where, at this very moment, his soul was crouching like a lithe and supple feline at bay.

Yet when he thought back to this passage now, he felt quite differently about it.

He was filled with a delightfully reassuring sensation, as if he had felt the touch of a firm, well-meaning hand on his shoulder. In an instant his mind was made up. An idea came to him in a flash, and he seized on it without hesitation, as if under the influence of his parents' exhortations.

He stayed awake until the other three came back, and waited until their soft, regular breathing told him they were asleep. Then, quickly tearing a page out of his notebook, by the faltering glow of the night lamp he scribbled a message in large, garbled letters:

In the morning they're going to hand you over to the class, and you can expect the worst. The only way out is to go to the Headmaster and confess what you did. He'll hear about it eventually anyway, but by that time you'll have been virtually beaten to death.

Put the blame on B. and R. and don't mention me.
You can see now that I do want to save you.

He slipped the note into the sleeping Basini's hand. And then, exhausted by all this emotional agitation, he too fell asleep.

20

THE NEXT MORNING, Beineberg and Reiting appeared to want to grant Törless another day's grace.

For Basini, however, things were taking a turn for the worse.

Törless saw Beineberg and Reiting going from one person to another, and then groups gathering round them in which everyone was whispering excitedly.

He still didn't know whether Basini had got his note, but sensing that he was being constantly watched, he had no opportunity to speak to him.

At first he was afraid that he was going to be implicated as well. But faced with the repulsive nature of the threat, he was now so paralysed that he would have simply let it engulf him.

Only after a while, timidly, expecting them to turn on him at any second, did he join one of the groups. But no one even noticed him. For the moment it was Basini who was the centre of attention.

The unrest began to grow. Törless could see it happening. It was more than possible that Reiting and Beineberg had fabricated some of the evidence...

At first there were grins, then a few people began to look serious, and angry glances were directed at Basini, until eventually an obscure, smouldering silence laden with dark desires hung over the class.

By coincidence it was a free afternoon.

They all gathered at the back of the classroom, in front of the lockers; then someone was sent to fetch Basini.

Beineberg and Reiting stood either side of him like a pair of animal tamers.

Once the doors had been locked and lookouts posted, the tried-and-tested ritual of making him undress caused much amusement.

Reiting produced a bundle of letters written by Basini's mother to her son, and began to read them out.

"My good little boy…"

General hilarity.

"You know that, as a widow, I have very few funds at my disposal…"

A chorus of unrestrained laughter and obscene jokes rose from the crowd. Reiting was about to carry on when someone gave Basini a shove. Half in jest, half in outrage, another boy pushed him back again. And then all of a sudden, his mouth contorted with fear, the naked Basini was spinning from one side of the room to the other like a football, amid roars of laughter, cheers, prods and punches, cutting himself on the sharp edges of the desks, falling over and skinning his knees, until finally he collapsed in a heap, bleeding, covered in dust, his eyes glazed over like a frightened animal. For a moment there was silence, and then everyone rushed over to look at him lying on the floor.

Törless shuddered. He had just witnessed the terrifying power of the threat.

And still he had no idea what Basini was going to do.

It was decided that the next night Basini would be tied to a bed and flogged with fencing foils.

But to everyone's amazement, during first lesson the next morning the Headmaster walked in. With him were the form master and two other members of staff. Basini was taken out of class and put in a separate room.

The Headmaster then berated them about the brutal behaviour that had just been brought to his attention, and said there would be a thorough investigation.

Basini had come forward and admitted what he had done.

Someone had obviously warned him about what was going to happen.

No one suspected Törless. He just sat quietly, wrapped up in his thoughts, as if the whole business had nothing to do with him.

Not once did it occur to Reiting and Beineberg that he might be the traitor. In fact they had never taken the threats they had made to him seriously: they had only done it to intimidate him, to show their superiority, or perhaps their anger; but now that had passed they barely gave it a thought. In any case, their obligations to Törless's parents would have been enough to stop them from taking any action against him. For them this was such a matter of course that they would never have imagined him capable of the slightest intrigue.

Törless had no regrets about what he had done. Its clandestine and cowardly aspects didn't matter compared with the feeling of total liberation that it had brought him. After all the turmoil everything was miraculously clear and uncluttered, like a vast open space.

He didn't join in with the animated conversations that were going on around him about what might happen; he spent the day in a state of peace and tranquillity.

As evening drew in and the lamps were lit, he sat at his desk with the exercise book in which he had noted down his brief observations in front of him.

But he didn't spend much time reading them. He ran his fingers over the pages, and it seemed as if a delicate fragrance was rising off them, like the scent of lavender from old letters. It was the nostalgia mingled with tenderness that we show for a past that is dead and buried when, in the soft, pale shadows that it casts, and which seem to hold everlasting flowers in their hands, we rediscover a long-forgotten resemblance to ourselves.

These delicate, melancholy shadows, this pale fragrance seemed to fade into a vast, warm, rolling stream – the life that now opened up before Törless.

A stage in his development had come to an end, his soul had acquired another ring as a young tree does every year – and this silent, overwhelming sensation justified everything.

He began to leaf through his memories. The phrases with which he had confusedly recorded what had happened – the various and astonishing events into which life had plunged him – seemed to come alive, move about and take on coherent form. It was as if a shining path lay before him, one that bore the traces of his first tentative steps. And yet something seemed to be missing – not new ideas, of course, but it wasn't yet vivid enough to really seize hold of him.

He began to feel unsettled. And then anxious, because the next day he would have to stand in front of the masters and justify himself. But how? How could he explain all this? The dark, mysterious path that he had followed. When they asked him "Why did you ill-treat Basini?" could he really reply: "Because I was interested in the mental impression it would have on me, something that I still know very little about, and compared with which all my thoughts seem to be irrelevant"?

This last small step, which he needed to take in order to reach the end of the intellectual process, terrified him as if he were standing on the edge of a bottomless pit.

And before night had fallen he found himself in a state of feverish, anxious agitation.

21

T HE NEXT DAY, WHEN THE PUPILS were called in individually to be questioned, Törless had disappeared.

He had last been seen the previous evening, sitting at his desk with an exercise book that he seemed to be reading.

A search was made of the entire school; Beineberg took a discreet look in the attic, but Törless was nowhere to be found.

At that point it became clear that he had run away, and so the local police were notified and asked to bring him back in as tactful a way as possible.

In the meantime the investigation had begun.

Reiting and Beineberg, who were convinced that Törless had run away because they had threatened to implicate him, felt duty-bound to divert any suspicion from him, and spoke up strenuously in his defence.

They shifted all the blame onto Basini, and one after another the whole class came in and testified that Basini was a good-for-nothing thief, whose response to their well-meaning attempts to make him mend his ways was to keep committing the same crimes. Reiting insisted that while they realized they had acted wrongly, they had only done it out of compassion, because they felt that one shouldn't report a classmate until all the various friendly warnings had been tried; and the entire class swore for a second time that their ill treatment of Basini was just an outburst of rage, because he had repaid their magnanimity with contempt and base behaviour.

In a word it was an act of collusion, brilliantly stage-managed by Reiting, and which, in order to justify their behaviour, struck every moral chord to which they knew the masters were susceptible.

Basini maintained an impassive silence. Since the day before he had been in a state of mortal terror, and his isolation in a separate room and the calm, orderly process of the inquiry were a release for him. He wanted nothing more than for everything to be over quickly. Not only that, Reiting and Beineberg hadn't neglected to threaten him with the most appalling revenge if he spoke out against them.

And then Törless was brought back. He had been found in the nearby town, dead on his feet and starving.

His reasons for running away now seemed to be the only mystery left in the whole affair. But circumstances were in his favour. Beineberg and Reiting had done a good job in preparing the ground, and had mentioned how excitable he had been lately, the moral sensitivities which had caused him to commit the crime of not immediately reporting something that he had known about from the start, thus making himself partly responsible for this calamity.

So Törless was met with a certain tender-hearted benevolence, which his friends were quick to alert him to beforehand.

Nonetheless he was still extremely agitated, and the fear of not being able to make himself understood left him completely drained…

For reasons of discretion, as there was still a fear that there might be more revelations to come, the investigation was held in the Headmaster's private apartments. Apart from him, the form master, the school chaplain and the mathematics tutor were also present, the last of whom, being the most junior member of staff, having been given the task of taking the minutes.

Asked why he had run away, Törless didn't reply.

All the heads nodded sympathetically.

"Don't worry," said the Headmaster, "that has already been explained to us. But tell us what made you decide to keep Basini's misconduct a secret?"

Törless could have lied. But his nervousness had left him. He had an irresistible urge to talk about himself and to try out his ideas on these people.

"I'm not quite sure, sir. When I first heard about it, it seemed to be something absolutely appalling... quite unimaginable..."

The chaplain gave him a satisfied and encouraging nod.

"I... I was thinking of Basini's soul..."

The chaplain's face lit up, the maths tutor wiped his pince-nez, put them back on, screwed up his eyes...

"I couldn't imagine the moment when a humiliation of that kind had befallen Basini, and it was this that kept drawing me closer to him..."

"All right – but what you are probably trying to say is that you felt a perfectly natural revulsion for your class-mate's lapse, and that the sight of vice mesmerized you, so to speak, in the way the eyes of a serpent are said to transfix its victim."

The form master and the maths tutor wasted no time in expressing their hearty approval of this allegory.

But Törless replied: "No, it wasn't exactly revulsion. It was... At first I just thought he had behaved badly and that he ought to be reported to those with the authority to punish him..."

"That is what you should have done."

"...But then I started to see him in such a peculiar light that I forgot all about punishment, and I realized that my opinion had completely changed; and whenever I thought of him in this way it was as if a crack had opened up inside me..."

"You must try and express yourself more clearly, my dear Törless."

"I can't explain it in any other way, sir."

"Come now, you're agitated, we can see that – confused, in fact. What you just said is extremely vague."

"Yes, it's true that I'm confused – I could have put it more clearly. But it always comes back to the same thing, that there was something extremely strange inside me..."

"I don't doubt that – but given the circumstances it's perfectly understandable."

Törless thought for a moment.

"Perhaps one could put it like this: there are certain things which in a sense are destined to have an effect on our lives in two different ways. In my case these are people, events, dark, dusty corners and a high, cold, silent wall that suddenly comes alive..."

"For Heaven's sake, Törless, what are you talking about now?"

But Törless was enjoying being able to say what was on his mind.

" ...imaginary numbers..."

They all looked at each other, and then at Törless. The maths master gave a little cough:

"I ought just to add here, to help clarify this somewhat obscure statement, that young Törless came to see me one day to ask me to explain some of the basic concepts of mathematics – particularly imaginary numbers – which can cause real difficulties for an untrained mind. I would go so far as to say that he displayed undeniable acuity, although he had almost an obsession for finding what – to him at least – seemed to be a gap in the causality of human thought, so to speak. Do you remember what you said to me, Törless?"

"Yes. I said that it seemed that in these instances thought wasn't enough in itself to allow us to make progress, and that we needed another certainty, an inner one, which would in a sense bridge the gap. And that was what I felt in Basini's case too – that thought alone wouldn't help."

The Headmaster was beginning to lose patience with these philosophical digressions, but the priest was delighted with Törless's response.

"So," he asked, "do you feel more drawn to the religious viewpoint than that of science?" And he turned to the others. "It was clear to me that it was very similar with Basini. He appears to be highly receptive to the most elevated, I might even say the divine, transcendent aspects of morality."

The Headmaster now felt obliged to go into this in more detail.

"Well, Törless, is it true what the Reverend Father says? Do you have a tendency to look beyond things and events – as you said in a rather roundabout fashion – in order to find a religious influence?"

He would have been very glad if Törless had finally given a straight answer, one that would have allowed him to base his verdict on solid evidence. But Törless answered: "No, it wasn't that either."

"So will you tell us once and for all, clearly and plainly, exactly what it was!" exclaimed the Headmaster. "This isn't the time or place to get involved in a philosophical debate!"

But Törless was now in a defiant mood. He sensed that he hadn't expressed himself very well, and yet the opposition as well as the misplaced approval that he had encountered gave him a sense of superiority over these older people, who appeared to know so little about the inner life.

"I can't help it if what I've said isn't what you thought I meant. I can't describe exactly what I felt each time; but if I tell you what I think about it now, then perhaps you will understand why it has taken me so long to free myself from it."

He stood proud and erect, as if it were him who were the judge, his gaze directed over their heads; he couldn't bear to look at these preposterous characters.

Outside the window a crow was sitting on a branch; apart from that, all that could be seen was a vast white expanse.

Törless sensed that the moment had come to speak clearly, unambiguously and confidently about the things inside him, which at first had been ill defined and agonizing, and then later weak and lifeless.

It wasn't that this certainty and clarity came from any new thoughts, but as he stood there, bolt upright, as if he were in an empty space, he could feel it, he could feel it with his whole being, just as he had before when he let his astonished gaze wander over his classmates while they were busy writing and doing their prep.

For thought is a strange phenomenon. Often it is nothing more than an accident that vanishes without a trace, because for thought there is a time to be born and a time to die. We can make an amazing discovery, and yet it slowly withers away in the palm of our hand like a flower. The form remains, but its colour and fragrance have gone. Or, put another way, we might remember it word for word, the logical value of its phrases might remain intact, and yet it drifts aimlessly on the surface of our being and we don't feel enriched by it. Until the moment – perhaps many years later – when it suddenly reappears, and we realize that in the interim we have been barely aware of its existence, although logically speaking we knew it all the time.

Yes, there are dead thoughts and living thoughts. The thought that moves around on the surface, in the light, and which can be regained by the threads of causality at any time, isn't necessarily the most vivid. A thought we encounter in this way remains as insignificant to us as a random soldier in a column of marching troops. A thought that might have passed through our mind a long time ago only really comes alive at the moment when something which isn't thought, which isn't logic is added to it, with the result that we feel its truth, independent of any proof, like an anchor that has been dropped into living, bleeding flesh... Only half of any great discovery is made in the light-filled region of the mind, the other half is found in the dark soil of our inner depths, and this is above all a state of mind which grows at the farthest extremity of our thoughts like a flower.

Törless only needed to experience a violent emotional shock in order for this final, pressing desire to find its way to the surface.

Paying no attention to the looks of consternation on all the faces, and as if purely for himself, he gathered his thoughts and began to speak without pausing, his gaze fixed on the horizon.

"Perhaps I haven't learnt enough yet to be able to express myself properly, but nonetheless I would like to describe what happened. I felt it in me again just a second ago. The only way I can explain it is to say that I see things in two different forms. Not only things, but thoughts as well. If I make an effort to distinguish between them, then they are the same today as they were yesterday, yet if I close my eyes then I see them in quite a different light. Perhaps I was mistaken about imaginary numbers; if I think about them in a mathematical context, so to speak, then they seem quite natural, but if I look at them in all their strange singularity they become inconceivable. But I may be mistaken, because I know so little about them. But I wasn't mistaken about Basini, I wasn't mistaken when I thought I could hear a faint murmuring on the high wall, when I couldn't stop staring at the silent, living dust lit up by the beam of a lamp. No, I'm not mistaken when I say that things have another, secret life that goes unnoticed! I... I don't mean it literally: I'm not saying that these things are actually alive, or that Basini has two faces – but that there is something else in me that doesn't see all this with the eyes of reason. Just as I can sense when a thought is being born in me, I can also sense that whatever it is inside me comes to life at the sight of certain things, and when my thoughts have fallen silent. There is something dark and obscure in me, which lies beneath all my thoughts, which I am unable to quantify in rational terms, a life that can't be described in words, and which nonetheless is still my life...

"This life of silence has oppressed me, exhausted me; I was unable to take my eyes off it. I was afraid that this was what our whole life might be like, that I would only ever experience it in odd, occasional snatches... oh yes, I was terribly afraid... completely distraught..."

In his highly agitated state of mind, these words and comparisons, which were very advanced for someone his age, seemed to come to him easily and naturally, in what was almost a moment of poetic inspiration. Then he lowered his voice and, as if still in the throes of angst, he added:

"...But that's all in the past. I realize that I was mistaken after all. I'm not afraid of anything now. I know that things are just things and that is what they will always be; and that I will continue to see them first one way and then another. Sometimes with the eyes of reason, sometimes in other ways... And I will stop trying to make comparisons between them..."

After that he said nothing more. And he felt that this was the right moment to leave, and in fact when he walked out no one tried to stop him.

When he had gone, the masters all looked at each other in amazement.

The Headmaster just shook his head, nonplussed. The form master was the first to find his tongue. "Well! This young prophet was trying to lecture us. But I'm damned if I could make head or tail of it. He was almost beside himself! And the way he got himself in a complete muddle over the simplest things!"

"Highly suggestible, purely extemporaneous ideas," agreed the mathematician. "It appears that he has attached far too much importance to the subjective elements of human experience, hence his confusion and all those obscure comparisons."

The chaplain didn't say anything. Törless had used the word "soul" so often that he would have liked to take the young man in hand. But he still didn't really know what he had been talking about.

It was the Headmaster who brought matters to a close:

"I have no idea exactly what's going on in Törless's head, but he has got himself into such a state of overexcitement that it wouldn't be appropriate for him to remain at the school any longer. His spiritual and intellectual nourishment requires the sort of careful nurturing that we are not in a position to provide. I don't feel we can accept the responsibility from now on. Törless is better suited to private tuition: that is what I shall recommend when I write to his father."

The others lost no time in agreeing with the Headmaster's well-intentioned suggestion.

"He really is most peculiar," remarked the maths tutor to the person next to him. "I wouldn't be at all surprised if he had hysterical tendencies."

At the same time as his parents received the Headmaster's letter, one also arrived from Törless, in which he asked them to take him away from the school, because he no longer felt it was the right place for him.

22

I N THE MEANTIME Basini was expelled, and life at the school returned to its usual routine.

It had been agreed that Törless's mother would come and collect him. He said goodbye to his classmates with a feeling of indifference. He had almost forgotten their names already.

He had never gone up to the red-painted room in the attic again. All that seemed far, far behind him now.

Now Basini had gone, it had died a natural death. It was almost as if the person who had been at the centre of the whole affair had taken it away with him.

A form of calm tinged with doubt descended on Törless, although the feelings of despair had left him. "It was probably the things I did in secret with Basini that made it worse," he thought. He couldn't imagine there being any other reason.

And yet he felt ashamed. In the way we are ashamed when we wake up in the morning after a night spent in the clutches of fever, during which we saw terrifying threats loom up from every corner of the darkened room.

His behaviour in front of the committee now struck him as utterly ridiculous. All that fuss over nothing! So perhaps they were right? And yet there was something in him that blunted this feeling of shame. "I probably behaved unreasonably," he thought, "although this whole business seems to have had very little to do with reason." This was how he felt about it now. He could still remember the storm that had raged in his head, which couldn't begin to be explained by the reasons he found in himself. "In that case," he concluded, "it must have been something far too vital and deep-seated to be judged in terms of reason and concepts."

Yet what had come before this outburst of passion, and which had simply been overshadowed by it – that was the real problem, and it hadn't gone away. It was the mental perspective that he had experienced, which varied according to the distance he was from something: that incomprehensible connection which, according to the point of view from which we see them, gives objects and events a value that sets them apart, makes them incomparable, alien to each other...

He saw this and everything else with a curious and perfect clarity – in every tiny detail. In the way we see things at daybreak, when the sun's first pure rays have dried the cold sweat of our fears, and our table, wardrobe, enemies and fate shrink back to their normal dimensions.

Nor was he spared the faint, brooding weariness that this leaves in its wake. He now knew the difference between night and day; in fact he had always known, although an oppressive dream had swept over the borderline between them, causing it to blur, and this confusion filled him with shame. And yet the thought that this could happen, that there were fragile, easily obliterated boundaries around people through which the febrile dreams that prowl around the edges of the soul are able to gnaw and open up strange, sinister pathways – this thought had embedded itself deep inside him, from where it cast pale, wan shadows.

This was not something that he could readily explain. But the inability to find the right words was an exquisite sensation, like the certainty of the expectant mother who feels the gentle tug of the future in her blood. And this confidence and lassitude were mingled together in him...

And so it was that, in a state of quiet, thoughtful serenity, he awaited the day of departure.

His mother, who had expected to find an overexcited, distraught young man, was struck by his cool composure.

As they drove to the station, on the right-hand side they passed the little wood where Božena's house stood. It looked so innocent and insignificant now, just a dusty tangle of willows and alders.

It reminded him of how inconceivable his parents' existence had seemed to him at the time. And he gave his mother a surreptitious glance.

"What is it, my boy?"

"Nothing Mama, I was just thinking."

And he inhaled the faint, gentle fragrance that drifted up from the bodice of her dress.

Note on the Text

This translation is based on *Die Verwirrungen des Zöglings Törleß* (Hamburg: Rowohlt, 2012). The chapter divisions have been introduced for clarity and ease of reading, as has been the practice in other translations of the novel.

Translator's Afterword

Among the many contributions that Central Europe has made to literature, the Bildungsroman is the form that it has in a sense made its own. The region's position at the geographical and cultural heart of Europe, where borders, regimes, language and national identities have for centuries been in a state of flux, creates an atmosphere in which coming of age – a difficult time of life in any part of the world – can be particularly torturous, beset by external influences that are as complex and ill defined as the inner life of the adolescent.

The Confusions of Young Master Törless (*Die Verwirrungen des Zöglings Törleß*), Robert Musil's first novel, is one of the earliest and most influential examples of the genre, an austere and yet pointillist tale that examines aspects of human nature that at the time were taboo subjects, and which to a certain extent still have the power to unsettle. What marks *Törless* out for greatness is that the themes with which it deals have subsequently become perennial, not only in literature but also in philosophy, sociology, psychology, social movements and the cinema, and continue to have a profound effect on our fundamental understanding of ourselves and of human relationships.

In essence, *Törless* is a story about adolescence, the age at which we become acutely and often painfully aware of ourselves and the world around us – a world viewed through the distorting lens of self-doubt, which can create monsters that will accompany us throughout our lives, with often far-reaching consequences for ourselves and for society. Yet Musil goes further, picking up the threads of a complex subject and following them into areas whose importance would not be recognized until much later, due in no small measure to his contemporaries Sigmund Freud and Carl Gustav Jung. He explores the themes of androgyny, young male beauty, the first stirrings of tenderness, the delicate vulnerability of adolescent boys, and how this conflicts with their displays of what they and many people even today regard as "masculine behaviour". Similar ideas regularly appear in Thomas Mann's work, notably *Tonio Kröger*, *The Confessions of Felix Krull* and *Death in Venice*, in Hermann Hesse's *Narcissus and Goldmund*, as well as in the Slovene writer Florjan Lipuš's *The Confusions of Young Tjaž* and Friedrich Torberg's *Young Gerber* – all novels in which sensitive and intelligent adolescent boys are manipulated and often destroyed by the brute ugliness of the world. More recently, the controversy provoked by Germaine Greer's book *The Boy* serves to remind us that society's attitudes to the reality of homoerotic feelings and the attraction felt for adolescent boys by both sexes has changed remarkably little since the scandal caused by Musil's novel in 1906.

For *Törless* is undoubtedly a homoerotic book (Basini has "a beautiful physique", not unlike that of a girl), set as it is in a boys' boarding school, where the place of the female is traditionally taken by attractive junior boys, a perverse landscape whose reality is rendered all the more contorted by the position accorded to women (Törless's sensitive friend, the young Prince H., is regarded by the others as "soppy" and "effeminate", while Basini – himself the largely willing focus of his classmates' desires – tells Božena, a local prostitute, that women "aren't fit for anything else"). The narrative constantly draws our attention to the atmosphere of tumescent longing in the grim establishment – whose isolated position is apparently designed to insulate pupils from the "bad influences" of the city – inhabited by hundreds of adolescents whose senses are finely tuned to the slightest sexual innuendo.

Yet the longings that the boys feel are not only sexual or sentimental. Musil later claimed that his choice of subject matter was incidental, and that he could have developed any number of other "perversions" and taken them to their logical conclusion. The carefully orchestrated bullying campaign, the sexual abuse of Basini, are just part of a much wider, more commonplace and, as a result, far more sinister phenomenon: the abuse of power. It is in this respect that the novel acquires the parabolic quality that some people have interpreted as predicting the Great War and the subsequent rise of Fascism – although to any observant European of the time (and this can be seen in Mann's *Death in Venice* with its cast of pursued Poles and overbearing Russians and Germans, as well as in the scandal caused by the Colonel Redl affair), it was clear that the "old" Europe was disintegrating under the pressure of malign influences.

To anyone who, like Musil, was educated at such a school or at a military academy, or served in a fashionable regiment, the setting and atmosphere of the novel will be instantly and perhaps uncomfortably familiar. In a sense, the four main protagonists represent the different, conflicting elements of the adolescent character: Beineberg is a cold, pseudo-intellectual manipulator, Reiting a compulsively ambitious and seductive orator and Basini – temptation incarnate – a pleasure-seeking flirt (and arguably the person who is most honest with himself), while Törless is the sceptic, the misguided fool who questions and agonizes – in fact he could be described as the collective conscience who, in Musil's unfinished chef-d'œuvre *The Man without Qualities,* develops into the cynical seducer, Ulrich.

As is often the case, Törless is an outsider, partly by choice; he desperately wants to belong, but on his own terms. He is drawn to the cloistered life, but it rejects him. What he is really seeking is a cloister within a cloister, his own private milieu. But, as usually happens, his youthful attempts to find it end in failure, and yet also in greater self-awareness.

Much of the novel's impact derives from Musil's poetic and incisive prose, an incomparable blend of *Schönbrunner Deutsch*, the version of German spoken at the Habsburg Court (and indeed still used by some elements of Austrian and particularly Viennese society, where girls say *küss die Hand* – "I kiss your hand" – to greet their mothers, and young men routinely click their heels to their elders and seniors) – littered with idioms from French and the many different national languages of the Empire – and *Kanzleisprache,* the intricately formal parlance of the omnipresent Austro-Hungarian bureaucracy. As a result the narrative often resembles a combination of an epic poem and a ministerial briefing document, leading us through a maze of subordinate clauses where foreign words and phrases suddenly explode like fireworks.

The subtle and sometimes labyrinthine idiosyncrasies of Musil's language were instrumental in choosing the title of this new translation – *The Confusions of Young Master Törless*. The word *Zögling* from the original German title has never been properly reflected in English. At the time the novel was written, the term described a pupil at a boarding school, deriving from the verb *ziehen* ("to draw along" or "draw up") and also possibly from *züchten* ("to breed"), with its attendant aristocratic associations. Since then, however, *Zögling* has largely fallen out of use, acquiring a humorous or ironic sense which today might be used to describe someone who (like Törless) has aristocratic pretensions. Hence "Young Master Törless" seemed a suitably ironic English rendering – although true equivalents rarely exist in translation.

Despite the passage of time, the novel has lost none of its ability to unsettle, to make us reflect on the darker and more troubling aspects of human nature and the violent excesses to which they can lead – and, even in the enlightened twenty-first century, one doesn't have to look far to find examples. Children are still routinely abused, bullying is still widespread at every level of society, people misuse power for their own ends and wars are fought for the most specious ideological reasons or simply to bolster the egos of insecure dictators. Yet when such institutionalized crimes are exposed, those who uncover them (or "blow the whistle") are often condemned as traitors.

So has anything really changed? Adolescent boys still suffer from the same angst experienced by Törless, unaware that their fragile beauty is as ephemeral as their self-doubt. As Thomas Mann wrote in *Tonio Kröger*: "I stand between two worlds. I am at home in neither, and in consequence I suffer."

It is still a world that Robert Musil would recognize.

– Christopher Moncrieff

Christopher Moncrieff translates widely from French, German and Romanian literature. After military service in Europe, the Near East and the USA during the Cold War, he produced large-scale *son et lumière* shows in Germany, France and Los Angeles before beginning to write and translate. He read Theology at Oxford and has qualifications in design and on the military staff. A frequent traveller in Central and Eastern Europe, he speaks a number of the languages of the region.

ALMA CLASSICS

<small>ALMA CLASSICS</small> aims to publish mainstream and lesser-known European classics in an innovative and striking way, while employing the highest editorial and production standards. By way of a unique approach the range offers much more, both visually and textually, than readers have come to expect from contemporary classics publishing.

LATEST TITLES PUBLISHED BY ALMA CLASSICS

To order any of our titles and for up-to-date information about our current and forthcoming publications, please visit our website on:

www.almaclassics.com